A Compass for the Sunflower

A Compass for the Sunflower

Liana Badr

Translated from the Arabic by
Catherine Cobham

The Women's Press

First published in Great Britain by
The Women's Press Limited 1989
A member of the Namara Group
34 Great Sutton Street, London EC1V 0DX

Originally published in Arabic as *Bosla Min Ajl ʿAbbād Al-Shams* by Ibn Rushd, Beirut, 1979

British Library Cataloguing in Publication Data
Badr, Liana
A compass for the sunflower.
I. Title
892′.736[F]
ISBN 0 7043 5037 8

Typeset by AKM Associates (UK) Ltd,
Southall, London
Reproduced, printed and bound in Great Britain by
BPCC Hazell Books Ltd
Member of BPCC Ltd
Aylesbury, Bucks, England

The translator wishes to
thank Shahla Suleiman for her help.

Translator's Note

The narrative of *A Compass for the Sunflower* moves backwards and forwards in time and space between several episodes of recent Palestinian history. For the reader unfamiliar with this history it may be useful to indicate briefly some of the key events referred to.

The Arab–Israeli War of June 1967 brought the Palestinian inhabitants of East Jerusalem, the West Bank and Gaza under direct Israeli military rule. Many Palestinians, and in this novel Jinan and her family, left their homes on the West Bank for the East Bank of the Jordan expecting to return shortly afterwards when the Israeli army had been defeated, just as many Palestinians had left their homes within the pre-1967 Israeli borders during the 1948 war.

In September 1970, also known as Black September, the Jordanian regime crushed the Palestinian resistance and expelled its remnants from Amman and later from the country as a whole. The Jordanian regime had kept a close watch on the Palestinian activists on the West Bank in the period up to 1967, a surveillance punctuated by periods of outright repression, such as when Jinan's father was arrested, presumably in the late 1950s.

After Black September the centre of the Palestinian resistance shifted to Lebanon and in particular to its capital Beirut, where there had been Palestinian refugee camps such as Sabra and Shatila since after the 1948 war. The episodes where Jinan is in Beirut (and Shahd stays in Amman and Thurayya returns to Nablus) take place in the early 1970s before the outbreak of the Lebanese civil war which began in 1975. Presumably the hijack described in the novel also takes place during this period, probably in the Jordanian desert.

1

Sabra in the morning: the market selling fresh fruit and vegetables to be exported in huge loads to the Gulf states; butchers hanging up carcasses and decorating them with bundles of parsley; dozens of empty handcarts waiting for traders to hire them to carry the day's merchandise; hen coops crammed with black and white chickens; and swarms of flies hovering over the heaped-up mounds of rubbish at the heads of the alleyways leading into the market. I breathed in the cold air which went sharply up my reddened nose as I looked at the feeble threads of light struggling through the grey clouds. Grey or blue or white, ever-present colours which change from moment to moment and only resemble one another in the memory. I stood on the pavement waiting for a service taxi to take me into the city. Big patches of grey mud stained the crumbling asphalt. And then I saw a pool of blood.

Blood! I turned in sudden surprise to look for the source of the red puddle and saw a butcher hanging up the animal he had just slaughtered. I averted my eyes. Blood mingling with the grey and blue and white, and springing up through the cracks of memory. You forget, then suddenly you glance behind.

A man came towards me, supporting a woman. Tenderness welled up from his arms, and the woman was like a plant growing from his body, branching outwards but hesitant to break away from the cramped pot. Her young, tired face, already lined by the years, sent a violent wave of emotion surging through me, triggered off by some memory I couldn't locate.

The service taxi had drawn up. I took my seat and was engulfed by a powerful smell of antiseptic coming from the woman as she too stepped into the taxi. I found myself looking involuntarily at the pool of blood mixed with mud and water. That feeling of heaviness descended on me, and I expected to hear the long-drawn-out cry of the little girl as she rolled on the cold tiles: I'd grabbed hold of her to stop her moving while the nurse went on stitching up her hands, which were full of tiny fragments of shell. Dark blood dripped from them and the needle went back and forth, pulling together the jagged edges of her torn, punctured flesh. She screamed out loud and I agonisedly tried to calm her down. There were no anaesthetics and we were carrying out operations in primitive conditions without proper equipment or medicines.

I waited to hear that resounding cry blending in with the harsh, grating sounds of stupefying pain, vocal chords torn in throats constricted by anguish and horror, and the thump of American howitzers, as the stale air grew ranker and thicker in the first aid centre of the Jabal Al-Hussein camp in Amman.

I waited but no cry came and there were only the familiar everyday noises of Beirut awakening from sleep and the sound of the service taxi rattling round a bend in the road or grumbling on the steep slopes.

2

I reached into my bag and took out my handkerchief. The warm powerful smell of jasmine rose from it. Flowers from Umm Mahmoud's plants. I picked the yellowed remnants of a crumpled flower off the handkerchief.

The day before, she'd said to me enquiringly, 'Shaher's very late this time, isn't he?'

'Yes. He is.'

But then, putting on a calm manner which bore no relation to how I felt, I'd said, 'Umm Mahmoud, we're used to him being away for a long time when he can't get leave.'

She gave me her pale smile, then turned to go out, saying, 'Let's hope you're right, daughter.'

Before she left the room she put the bouquet of jasmine on the table.

The chessboard building with its panes of dark glass reflected the buildings crowded around it. In the entrance I stopped at the enquiries desk. The official's eyes bored into me above his small thick moustache. Without waiting for my question, he said, 'No. No letters for you.'

Then he raised his eyebrows to confirm his negative reply and to show his surprise. 'That's a stubborn girl, and no mistake,' he would say as soon as I'd gone past him towards the big lift. 'If I had any letters for her, I'd give them to her.'

Lifts and flats, flats and lifts everywhere. Lifts for quick, secret love, and flats for a steady, settled way of life. And I had neither.

I got out the typewriter and began to tap the keys; the letters appeared on the white paper, proceeding rapidly from right to left, from east to west. East and west are two sides of an equation according to Amer, Salima Al-Hajja's son. Amer had come out of prison, and I'd had no news of him. But the same was true of Shahd: it was ages since any of her stories, written in a small, clear hand, had reached me; and Thurayya's letters, sent from the West Bank via Europe, were a long time coming. I'd expected a letter from my sister Sima at least.

I had a vision of Sima drinking in the desert landscape, the sand driven into spiralling eddies which blew fiercely along. I could see her glaring in anger at the sandstorm, discomfited by the hot, gritty particles which penetrated and covered everything, and wiping the dust off her school exam certificates, proud to be top of her class in the PLO's evening schools. Even when she complained her smile retained a purity that was a part of her face; the expression of an obstinate child who rebelled against everything.

I looked out of the window and saw the sky, clear and blue, white muslin or white clouds, there was no difference. The city appeared to be made of towering buildings many storeys high, steel skeletons covered in cement and concrete. When Shaher and I were in Amman we had a huge window. We would sit at it and stare at the shapes of the clouds and invent names for them. Shaher said, 'That's the wolf chasing Little Red Riding Hood. She looks like you. Look! It *is* you.'

Gaily, I disagreed: 'No, it looks like a white dog with shaggy hair.'

I gazed into the little world of warmth and affection in his eyes. 'I would have loved you even if you'd had ugly eyes,' I told him.

He laughed, then looked at me; his laughter was the most beautiful thing in my life.

'I'd have hated all women if I hadn't known you,' he said.

Slyly he went on, 'That cloud's a tall woman with black hair holding seashells in one hand and a brass coffee pot in the other . . . When are you going to make us some coffee?'

For days, months, years, we hadn't looked at the sky together. We closed the circle of time then sat on top of it, ill at ease, stealing glances at the white and blue and grey with a hidden yearning for the old days. My precise memory for trivial, unimportant dates amazed him.

'Are you a sunflower?' he asked me once.

I teased him back, grumbling loudly, 'Did you think I was an automatic clock that didn't work?'

'On my way here I noticed a stupid Arabic film called *No Time for Love*; it must be about us,' he said.

Now it was my turn to sound perplexed: 'Why do the tanks always come and eat up periods of our history? The only dates we remember are the Balfour Declaration, the Rogers visit and the carnage of Black September.'

He reached for a match and struck it, then said in a low voice, before he lit his cigarette, 'Because the exile has left firm, clear footprints. We mustn't forget them or, as Salima Al-Hajja says, we'll become gypsies roaming the earth in permanent exile.'

From time to time I looked at the sky to see what the weather was going to be like before I went to work, or to count the enemy aircraft passing high overhead. When they broke the sound barrier above the camp the noise plummeted down into the bowels of the earth, earth where tin-roofed houses and shacks and apartment buildings were crammed together, and thousands of children and millions of reptiles crawled. The jets left a coil of exhaust which changed rapidly into a large tapeworm dancing in a circle on the blue screen. Deaf Musa, the greengrocer, fixing the headcloth more firmly round his face, repeated in the tone of one who is acquainted with the inner mysteries of things, 'Their trails are hard to get rid of because they change into clouds.'

Samih, one of Umm Mahmoud's sons, interrupted scornfully, 'Just wait a few minutes and the exhaust will evaporate and disappear from the sky.'

I looked back at the city, a collection of grey walls all alike, intersecting and running parallel towards the sea and the mountain. I looked at the letters I was typing on the white paper and they were like a crossword puzzle. The letters multiplied in all directions under my fingers: this is the city of crossword puzzles and chessboards and apartment buildings and hamburger joints. Big squares emerged, divided up into various shapes by black partitions. Thurayya in Nablus; Shahd Al-Samadi in Amman; and Amer coming out of prison to be gathered up by Salima Al-Hajja and have her blessings and magic charms heaped upon him. The letters rushed here and there on the page. I felt slightly sick as the words streamed around me at speed, from right to left, from east to west. The bright sun spread over the concrete surfaces of the buildings and was absorbed into the windows and doors, a circle shrinking inside a vast square.

3

Once when I was a child I stared at the circle of light surrounding the moon. The neighbours' children were taking me home that night and I asked Shahd's sister what this luminous circle was called. She laughed in that vague way older people have and replied that it was called the aureole. A silver moon like an acid drop, then this yellow-white-blue circle round it. What if I picked up the moon and put it my pocket and all that remained in the sky was this halo of light? It was like the bald man in our neighbourhood who looked at me from his distant spot but didn't speak. He couldn't speak proper Arabic, so he didn't have a beautiful mouth, our Arabic teacher said. The moon rolled along in front of our shadows, which preceded us over the asphalt and filled us with terror. An overwhelming sense of happiness spilled over into our waving arms as we went in noisy procession, shouting and laughing uproariously, down the long empty street. At night we owned the citrus groves, the orchards, and the crows' nest toadstools growing in stealthy silence. The sound of frogs croaking rose up from the irrigation ditches running between the trees and plots of cultivated land. Ahmad, son of one of the fruit growers, said, 'Guess which is the voice of the female frog and which is the male's.'

'Stop that nasty talk!' scolded his older sister. 'It was bad enough hearing you telling dirty jokes to your friends today.'

Ahmad was silent and I savoured the full measure of the freedom in our dancing, waving hands as they reached up under the citrus trees. I was taken by surprise to see my father coming towards us in the company of strangers, dark men wearing long coats in springtime. Our procession came to a halt and I said to him with a smile full of astonishment, 'Where's Mummy?'

He was silent for a moment then said in a tone of voice which was new to me, 'She's waiting for you at home.'

A vague terror stirred in me and I asked, 'And where are you going now?'

The men tried to hurry him and an unpleasant feeling of aversion towards them made me ill at ease. My father allayed my fears with his gentle manner of speaking. 'She's waiting at home. I'm just going to walk around a little, then I'll be back.'

I was somewhat reassured by this information. I noticed my mother's reddened eyes and altered colour as she opened the door. A feeling of sorrowful constraint stopped me from asking her if she'd been crying. I guessed that she was upset by something I couldn't understand and was unable to defend her from. To comfort her I lied, and said that my father was going to have a nice time with those men for a bit then come home. She didn't speak but abruptly took me in her arms, then led me off to bed. I closed my eyes, but went on listening to the sounds of her opening and shutting drawers and cupboards, unearthing things I hadn't known existed before that night.

When I woke up in the morning, our life had changed in many ways. I found out that my father had been arrested, and that our beloved house with its vegetable garden and the stream where the grass sang whenever we ruffled it with our bare feet no longer belonged to us. After that, I don't remember exactly what happened. My father was away a long time and we lived in many different houses. Gone were the loquat trees whose unripe fruit we used to steal unrepentantly, though it always gave us stomach ache. Gone was the man who sold us delicious ice cream for half a piastre and the spectre of the decaying fingernails we could expect to find in it if we were to believe our families' warnings. What I remember very clearly is that I stopped searching in cracks in the ground for a waxy yellow flower with shiny leaves. That city we moved to after my father's arrest was not called Jericho.

4

I gathered up the pages I'd typed and propped them up at one corner of the desk whose surface was strewn with pens, rulers and the morning papers. Amongst them stood a little vase of water in which a kind of shade-loving plant was putting out horizontal roots; its green leaves reached up over the edge of the vase while small, transparent, withered fragments of leaves floated in the murky water, apparently stuck there in a solid sticky mass. I felt a wave of optimism at the sight of it, then abandoned any such superstitious feelings. For a fleeting moment I tried to remember when I'd started to believe in good and evil omens. Was it with the blue beads I'd worn round my neck as a child, the sign of the hand outstretched to poke out the evil eye, the horseshoes nailed on so many doors? Once we went on a trip to the countryside and I picked a bunch of beautiful pink flowers to give to my mother. She shouted at me, scolding, 'You stupid girl, why are you bringing me oleanders? They're the flowers they put on graves.'

And later I was forced to acknowledge that impulsive feelings, great thoughts and wonderful days could end, and I had to take her death as an example. I had waited many years for her to rise from the dead. If people did come back from the dead, she would have done it and she wouldn't have told me off for bringing her lovely pink flowers called oleanders. Shade-loving plants are known for their amazing ability to grow and divide. They need only a little water. But when they grow old nothing can halt their progress towards death and decay. Their blossoming has a strange, wild exuberance and soil is unimportant to them, although without it their growth can be neither normal nor continuous.

As the headlines of the daily paper caught my eye I thought, 'Newspapers aren't weighed down by sorrows, or moved by joys. For them, like for poor Napoleon, there's nothing new under the sun.'

What I saw next I found hard to believe: Amer in the doorway of a hijacked jumbo jet. I read on and found the usual details of the hijacking and of the hijackers' demands and the conditions set for the release of the hostages, a repetition of accounts of other hijack operations. But this time it was Amer. He'd shaved off the beard which he'd come back from France with after graduation. He had a degree in engineering and he'd thrown himself into his work until he was interned for taking part in the September fighting.

The women took cover behind their windows. The rumble of shells had stopped and the threat of having to surrender hung over the Jabal Al-Nuzha district of Amman. Sheikh Subhi, the district *mukhtar*, had signed a ceasefire agreement with the army when the fighters' ammunition ran out. Some of them had been able to pull out and the rest began looking for empty houses and abandoned shacks. Fear held sway in many of the houses and their occupants were reluctant to give shelter to the beaten men. The eye of the intelligence services was bigger than the eye of God, and the punishment for harbouring fighters was too terrible to contemplate.

A light sand-laden wind blew through the alleyways and the men clustered in small groups on scattered grubby blankets around empty tea glasses.

It was a time when I was incapable of thinking up any ideas to lighten the stifling atmosphere of the night as it crept between the slumbering houses. All I could do was offer them my packet of cigarettes and forgo the relief which smoking afforded to the burning inside me. Why did the words of welcome fade from people's lips just before the army overran the area? I looked towards Amman where a few small distant fires burned and thought bitter thoughts, as bitter as my dry mouth which had hardly been moistened with water in the past few days. Why do they have the idea that the world is so small? I thought fruitlessly. All Amman was pulsating with movement and the fall of a few areas didn't mean that the enemy's fist would block every single access. I recollected the sight of the fall of the Jabal Al-Hussein camp the day before.

Out of their tin-roofed houses, wrecked by the eight days of shelling, they drove thousands of men, women and children. They separated out the men; the women stood to one side in their long black dresses, their wailing and lamentations rising to form a dense cloud in the sky above the shattered camp, while the men and youths raised their arms high, like a vast forest of severed, broken trees. I lost all feeling and will as I witnessed a fantasy world of soldiers in torn khaki with gun muzzles levelled, bazookas hurtling to earth and American tanks driving to and fro. A jasmine bush laden with white blossoms exuded its warm fragrance redolent of moisture and shade, its delicate scent streaming in the air alongside the chill heat of the shrapnel and the suffocating sulphur dust mixed with the smell of shoe rubber and dried blood. They stripped the women of their jewellery and the children of the gold charms they wore. I knew just what they would be like: every household where there were children had these charms in the shape of gold hands with *What God has willed* engraved on them. Shots rang out from time to time and the echoes tore through the hot air.

The tears froze in my throat, which was already sore from the lumps of dry bread I'd been trying to swallow, and blocked my windpipe and stopped me breathing. The world slithered down into a sticky abyss as I saw them open the door of the first aid centre I'd left the day before, and the sound of shots rose up metallically one after another. So rapid was the exchange of rocket fire that the air took on the shape of an arc overhead. They killed them. The wounded died once and the dead were killed over again. Rockets fell all around and my tears ran down over the golden hand like balls of quicksilver and by themselves effaced the inscription, *What God has willed.*

'You won't be able to make the prison wardress dance again now, Jinan.'

The image of the police station in Jericho came suddenly into my mind; on its flagpole fluttered the flag of a king who bought his army as if they were a flock of black ewes and planted his spies to sniff people out and follow their trails. They summoned me and Shahd and we went wearing our green-striped school overalls. The interrogator shouted in a melodramatic tone of voice, 'Who was behind this demonstration? Own up, or you'll find out what I can do to you.'

I feigned scorn and indifference. He shouted in his hoarse, dry voice. 'You're a cheeky student, Jinan, with no respect for anyone, and you're behaving in a foolhardy and arrogant fashion. Your friend Shahd is more sensible than you and she has a better grasp of what's going on: she's already told us everything we wanted to know.'

I pretended to be stupid and said naively, 'What did she confess to? We don't know anything.'

I looked at her out of the corner of my eye and she responded by raising her eyebrows to indicate that she'd said nothing.

'These leaflets in your handwriting, copied on carbon paper, contain a call to participate in a demonstration to be held today, setting out from the mosque gate. Do you really think we're idiots and know nothing?'

That's right. You never spoke a truer word, Interrogator. But we're not going to confess, although I'm dying to know how you found out about us. By listening? You don't even know the meaning of the word. You're the only one who doesn't know your channels of information and it doesn't even bother you, and we all know as much as you but by a different route. He repeated with malicious satisfaction, 'The two of you are stupid. You don't understand anything. Who pushed you into this ill-advised escapade?'

To myself I answered, 'No one pushed us. It was something we had to do.'

But I went back to smiling inanely and without emotion, and provoked by my behaviour he roared, 'If you don't stop this nonsense I'll be personally responsible for your punishment. You deny the work of your own hands and then sit in front of me chewing gum.'

The fury in his tone grew more pronounced and he burst out threateningly in my face, 'Spit that gum out, or I'll give you a beating like you've never had in your life.'

The district chief arrived and joined in the abuse and threats, and told us that he wanted to have us expelled from school. By the end of our meeting the two men's foreheads were pouring with sweat. 'It's prison for you, then, irresponsible girls,' they said finally. 'You'll learn an invaluable lesson there. When you're in with those filthy women you'll regret your silence.'

They led us up to the cells on the floor above; the prison looked shabby and small to us, not like the prisons we'd seen at the cinema in Jericho at Friday matinées. We were received by a short, stout woman dressed in military uniform with the face of a hungry old man. She locked us in the cells then sat outside in the empty room staring at us. Shahd inveigled her into answering our questions about the harshness of prison life. We made small talk with her and learnt that she was Circassian and a first lieutenant. In a theatrical manner which did not seem to arouse the officer's suspicion, Shahd squealed, 'Circassian! How we love those songs they play on the radio every week!'

I let out a shriek of delight: 'And the Circassian dances are so exciting. God, I love them! I began to learn how to do them. Look . . .'

I stood up on the stone bench with Shahd and we began to go through the dance we'd learnt along with our regional dance, the *dabke*, and an Indian dance for the annual school concert. She showed her teeth in a faint, shy smile and started to give us directions and tell us what we were doing wrong. But then almost immediately she scowled and fell silent. Up the stairs we heard the sound of heavy military boots approaching. The boots' owners accompanied us back to the interrogator. We were going to be released on bail. 'Are you listening? It's a 300 dinar bail. It's not easy for your parents to pay a sum like this. The next time you won't be let out of prison for years, and school will be struck out of your lives.'

The next time. How many next times would we shrug off death and destruction after the refugees had left Jericho? So why didn't we benefit from the bail statements which the Jordanians left behind them intact in their miserable police station for our conquerors to avail themselves of?

Columns of fighters rushed towards the military vehicles. I was certain that Amer and dozens of others I knew were among them. If I hadn't had to go on a mission to Jabal Al-Nuzha I would have been with them now, perhaps in that armoured car crammed with young men and women dressed in dark green . . .

But the soldiers were on their way towards us and the wide sweep of land lay under siege from them and their machine guns from the opposite side. Our armour-piercing shells had run out, and the *mukhtar* had signalled to them secretly that they were safe to come.

5

The tapping of the typewriter was oddly regular, reverberating like a clock with a hoarse tick: many letters and a single, repeated sound; many days and a single, unbroken stretch of time, unvarying except when we put it in our pockets and held it tight in our trembling fingers afraid that it would slip down and be submerged deep in our memories. Shahd-the-Rain and Lily of the Valley, that's what I named her the day I saw her run into the garden after the rain and pick some blue flowers swaying in the breeze in the aftermath of the storm. She brought the flowers to our room at college and scattered them in every corner and on all the bookshelves and on the covers of our wooden beds.

'You're unashamedly romantic, Shahd!' I said.

'And why not?' She stretched her slender neck defiantly.

I waved a hand towards the books of revolutionary philosophy and said, 'But these teach us something different, don't they?'

She drew out a small red book and with a hint of uncertainty in her normally assured and commanding voice countered, 'But it's more beautiful like this. Don't you think so?'

And over its cover she shook out fragments of yellow pollen which clung together in little lumps because of the rain water. Replying to the covert challenge in her words I said, 'Better or worse? That's the question, not prettier or uglier, you pigheaded philosopher.'

Samar, curled up under the bedclothes with a headful of rollers, shouted, 'When are you two going to stop annoying me with your constant arguing? All good philosophers are asleep now, so leave them in peace.'

Her head drooped suddenly, her eyelids closed and she let out a long sigh.

Shahd Al-Samadi. Shahd-the-Rain and Lily of the Valley. Shahd was an English language teacher who'd become a secretary in a private firm after being banned from working in official schools and organisations. Now she worked as a teacher in the Wahdat refugee camp in Jordan and had written to me in Beirut describing a strange scene: workers from the cleansing department had come into the primary classes with DDT sprays; the little girls in the UNWRA school had rested their foreheads on the wooden desks with childish calm and acceptance, submitting without a murmur of protest as the powder was sprayed copiously over their hair. Wanting to sow the seeds of a new awareness in their silent eyes, Shahd told them many stories, until one day another teacher heard her as she was asking the girls what the word 'army' meant to them.

'Army means fire and gunpowder and wrecked houses,' they said.

'The army is a plague of locusts, Miss,' said one of them.

Round black eyes stared at her, flashing glances in her direction in the classrooms, on the stone staircases, from the corners of the small playground.

The principal said to her, 'This letter's for you.'

It was to tell her that she'd been dismissed and was signed by one of the intelligence officers who'd been following her around wherever she went since September.

Shahd-the-Dismissed-the-Expelled. As he played with the beads of his rosary, her uncle said with a spiteful laugh, 'So long as you refuse to behave any better, I'll be waiting just as eagerly as you to see what becomes of you.'

And his guffaws could be heard all the way to the mosque.

6

In my head is a group of shadowy squares. I scale their sides and climb on top of them. The green-clad trellis slips in about us as we sit in a café in the country on small rush chairs. His golden-brown eyes widen and I take another chair and sit right inside them. The green arms of the trellis reach out and its leaves emit loud whisperings. How much did I fall in love with you, Shaher, after I'd sworn to you that I would give up climbing the hills and rugged mountains of love? He touches my face with both hands and my body changes from a piece of dried-up rubber into a surge of fire and mud and water pouring over the old dam which had enclosed me in resentment and pain and destructiveness. I drink in wave after wave of the shudderings which suffuse my veins that were doomed before he came to a slow-burning wasting. A jolt, and another, then a third, and the compass quivers searching for the four points. An explosion of love. A burning heat and sap spreading through the stems. The two arms of the compass have no place; they are always either in the north or in the south. This is the face that I love, that I search for among the hundreds which are all around me every morning. A cool gentle breeze blows and you give me your jacket and I warm myself in it. I ask you, 'Can I possibly work with strangers again, people whom I belong to but who don't know me?'

I hear you speaking and forget to listen to the twittering of the birds of the valley flying above our heads. 'Why not? Beginnings aren't hard compared to the terror of endings. You're scared of them criticising you and gossiping about you. You can hold your own against them without any help. It's up to you where you stand.'

My hair, which I wore short like a boy's, and my eyes bare of make-up answered him. I said, 'I'm afraid they'll just see me as a frivolous woman who can come and go as she pleases.'

The philosophy professor used to look at me with annoyance and apprehension, and only speak to me when he had to. He changed his attitude to me after the final exam. Kant was a serious person who only believed in reason, and Thomas Aquinas was only interested in questioning theological ideas. But what about freedom? That's the problem of our times, isn't it? The professor brought me his book and wrote a dedication in it. The title of the book was *The Problem of Freedom.* He looked at me like an affectionate grandfather giving his granddaughter new chains to tie up her doll. 'I thought you were a spoilt child who wanted to attract attention by behaving in a stupid way,' he said, 'but I discovered a truthfulness in you and a steely endeavour.'

I remembered the director of the college reprimanding me for writing some lines from the 'Song of Songs' on the blackboard: 'Set me like a seal upon thine heart, a seal upon thine arm: for love is strong as death; and jealousy is cruel as the grave. . . I sought my beloved, but I could not find him . . . The watchmen that went about the city found me, they smote me, they wounded me; the keepers of the walls took away my veil from me. I charge you, O daughters of Jerusalem, if ye find my beloved, that ye tell him that I am sick of love.'

The director spoke extremely slowly in an attempt to make me take in what he was saying: 'We are living in an under-developed society and we are striving to attract as many young women as possible to our college. Think about the effect of the attitudes of liberated girls, girls who don't stop to consider what they do to the reputation of the college. I have every confidence in your intelligence, my daughter, so why not spare me the trouble of talking to you like this?'

In fact I was thinking about how I'd gone up to my room before presenting myself at his office, and put the Victory March from *Carmen* on the turntable, shouting loudly in time with it; then I'd put on more lipstick which they saw as a symbol of wantonness and seductiveness, disturbing the more sedate students, and I'd gone to him.

On another occasion the director caught me as I strolled one evening around the empty study buildings with Shahd. We'd brought a pot of glue with us and were sticking revolutionary posters on the neat clean walls. He looked at me with feigned surprise and let out a gasp intended to show his amazement at finding us alone there at a time when all students should have been eating their supper in the restaurant. He said to me, 'Wouldn't you agree that your dress is shorter than it ought to be, and that you don't really take your classes seriously? You seem to forget that your father is paying for you to come here with the sweat of his brow so that you can lay the foundations of a bright future for yourself.'

Yes, Director. I'm dealing with my future just as you're telling me to, but I don't perceive it with the sad, troubled eyes of you and the other teachers. Perhaps you heard about the storm I unleashed recently. Perhaps. Who knows. I was in the middle of a crowd of male and female students and a foreign woman journalist asked me, 'And you, do you attach importance to virginity?'

My reply was abrupt and shocking: 'No. It doesn't bother me.'

I heard a few mutterings around me for she had received different replies from the girls who were well versed in the principles of correct behaviour and protocol, and one of the male students had stressed that his girlfriend's past and her previous relationships were of no concern to him as long as her hymen was intact. When the journalist asked me about my plans and hopes for the future, I replied that destiny was not an individual matter and I would not be concerned for my own position since anything that I gained would be worthless if my people had lost everything. To the amazement of the other students who looked on with startled eyes, this left-wing journalist flung her arms around me and I sensed genuine support and affection in the embrace.

Yes, Shaher, in the end I resented my woman's body. I rejected it and no longer wore anything but khaki trousers. I came to know where I stood by taking part in a succession of activities: attending student training camps, collecting donations, explaining propaganda, distributing political leaflets. In our indefatigable eagerness we would stand at the main gate of the college, waving down every car that passed and giving the passengers our leaflets. Some applauded our enthusiasm while others hurled insults at us: young girls in the full flower of youth displaying themselves on the public highway to distribute leaflets which wouldn't change anything.

My first visit to Baq'a camp was a surprise to me. There were real fedayeen who drank cups of coffee full of grounds and sat up all night with no complaints about the cramped ugliness of their cafeteria, unlike our fellow students in the college. Their office was a small hut with a corrugated iron roof and, stuck to its bullet-riddled walls, photographs of young men who'd died as martyrs. Real fedayeen who would become martyrs, who didn't expostulate angrily for hours over the poor quality of the cooked dishes and the salads in the restaurant. There I got to know other students who gave up several hours of study to share in the bustle of activity with the willing workers who thronged the desert camp.

To be progressive was to divest ourselves of the corruption which had been growing on us since we were born and to be melted down into a new society. Society. The society born of the new revolution. Would I have to learn how to evaluate a lot of things more accurately or examine them more closely? Everyone talked about revolution and women's liberation, and about transforming the balance of class forces which had operated in the old society, and I, like the rest of them, believed in what was being argued for and threw myself into logical discussions and considered that a beautiful revolution was the outstanding achievement of the twentieth century.

Then the glances and stares began to throw up a transparent barrier, invisible to the naked eye; the gleam of desire trembled in many an earnest lip, and I disliked these looks of my comrades, male and female, when they came to resemble the disapproving frowns of our old professors. 'If you carry liberation too far, you won't convince anyone', they said. 'She has open friendships and isn't the least bit scared or shy.'

I didn't back down from tasting the food of love with a friend of mine even though he responded to the things I did with revolutionary phrases and burning jealousy. He destroyed the candle I gave him as a present and said that I was a tormented human being who couldn't be trusted. When I asked why, he said because I took personal decisions without involving him, behaved uninhibitedly towards everyone, careless of my own interests, and laughed with them regardless of what they'd previously thought of me. He told me what he thought of my assortment of friendships and criticised the levity with which I embarked on things without bothering to consult him. I was supposed to ask him about the colour of the shirt I wore, the density of the water I drank, the size of the fleeting smiles I gave people. He wanted me to be his property with the boundaries, as regards people he didn't like and behaviour he found unacceptable, precisely defined. You've got a split personality, he told me. You don't know what you want. Exactly, dear friend, and who does? I think about our friendship and your concern for me. It doesn't interest me to make long-term plans for engagement and marriage.

I remembered a sincere girlfriend of mine whispering to me heatedly, 'You should learn how to hang on to your boyfriend. It won't do you any good to have processions of admirers.'

I know you have my best interests at heart, but who said that I was thinking of processions of admirers, or that as soon as I see them I make plans to exploit them in a public limited company?

But Amer. It was as if the blood in my head, jolted by the news of the hijack operation, had been turned round and made to flow in a different direction. He'd worn jeans all the time and had been unshaven, but in the photograph he looked clean-shaven and urbane. He used to talk to me about the speeches he'd made, the mass meetings he'd addressed in exile even though the police had picked him up on numerous occasions. Nonchalantly he passed me photo after photo of pretty girls who looked like film stars, and told me proudly, 'They're all faithful to me, but I'm not faithful to a single one of them. When I come back for good I'll marry a girl who knows how to make sage tea and cook chicken in the oven with olive oil and onions.'

I laughed to myself but asked him gravely, full of understanding, 'Then what will you do about these girls?'

He shrugged his shoulders derisively and poked me in the ribs, 'That's their problem. Who asked them to get mixed up with a dark, sentimental young man from the East? The resemblance to Omar Sharif? I doubt it. More likely the magic of the revolution from the non-materialistic Orient, and the camel caravans and the oil wells!'

In Amman in September his degree certificate was fixed to the boundary wall of the prison, a new stick to beat him with. And the May uprisings in Paris? 'I took part in them with some of my friends over there,' he said. 'We smashed up cars and metro stations and broke bottles of bad wine. Do you know what ten-year-old wine tastes like? A friend of mine took me to her father's château not far from Paris. Pleasure cascaded around us in golden waterfalls when we pulled the cork from a bottle of vintage wine. The wine was the colour of blood and, time had thickened it so that it had turned into a dense sticky liquid with the taste of apples ripened on the tree for ten years. Did you know that red was the colour of pleasure? The colour of new revolutions and of the carpets that revolutionaries find in emperors' palaces when they take them over.'

Salima Al-Hajja and the hopes she pinned on magic and miracles: she never tired of visiting fortune-tellers and diviners in her desire to ensure that her son came back safe and sound. Shahd visited her a number of times and laughed at the folktales and myths and the abundance of old sayings that she came out with, but she was aghast the day Salima told her the story of the snake: a diviner had asked her to get hold of the body of a male hoopoe and hang it on her vine trellis. The smell of the dead bird aroused a snake hidden among the branches and it slithered over the vine towards the suspended corpse. Salima Al-Hajja was engrossed in darning some clothes when the greedy snake dropped into her unsuspecting lap. It was very heavy and she jumped to her feet, thinking that a large rat had attacked her. The snake slunk away, and Salima lost faith in all fortune tellers and diviners.

'Will you go back to them?' Shahd had asked, whereupon Salima had vowed by the shrine of Saint Khidr that she never would.

I remembered her anxiously, with foreboding, for even as her illnesses had multiplied she insisted on doing everything she'd done before as if she still enjoyed good health, working busily with her needle and selling her simple garments whilst she sang her old songs and rejected all offers of help. I could almost smell the strong tobacco she used to smoke, rolling her own cigarettes in Ottoman papers; it was a pungent aroma that made your head spin when you came into the room. She sat in the corner on her mattress, or cooked her most delicious food for us, then sat on the floor while we ate, never touching a mouthful herself. From our early childhood she would tell us stories to encourage us to eat, about the jinn who'd stopped appearing among the stone arches in the alleys of Hebron after electricity was installed there. The light scared the she-jinn with her elongated eyes and she gave up walking at nights under the big wide windows. The she-jinn was a woman of striking beauty who wore her coal-black hair loose on her shoulders, and wound her *abaya* round her waist, and roamed through the alleyways enticing men, deluding them into thinking that she was just an ordinary woman with her olive-green eyes. But men – in the name of God the Compassionate the Merciful – knew her at once, for there was no hiding those almond-shaped eyes, and they would run back to the cosy warmth and hundrum safety of their homes and families.

And so it happened, when they were only part of the way there, that they would give up the idea of going to the café where the narghile, the deck of cards and the backgammon table awaited them, and ask divine protection from the devil and the beautiful eyes and the entrancing figure.

At night we would invent excuses so as not to have to go to sleep and would steal in among the mattresses spread on the floor, and the cotton pillows embroidered with doves and little birds, enjoying the tales she told of her late husband. They were stirring tales of his tyrannical behaviour, his power and authority, his daily consumption of a pair of pigeons and a pair of chickens. Shamelessly, he would pursue the poor women of the village tempting them with his wealth and his affluent lifestyle. Salima Al-Hajja revealed to us how she'd made a pact with his other wife to find out his secrets, secrets hidden behind moustaches the like of which no other man of his time could aspire to. But uncovering the conspiracies of the two women proved to be easier than cracking an old nut, and he drove her and the other wife into the field with his rifle, and made the two of them stay out there in the freezing cold under the walnut trees.

Excitedly we would ask her, 'And did you miss him after he was dead?'

Bowed down by the pain of her chronic asthma, she would

answer, 'It was very hard for me and for his other wife. Children, don't you understand that it is better to have even the shadow of a man than empty walls about you?'

None of us believed her, for she had told us how her youth was spent waiting for the next time he hit her with a stick which he always used to say to her was a branch cut from a tree growing in Paradise.

Shahd said, 'The city of Amman is like a messiah with wonderful sweet features, who sympathises with my sorrow although his hands are bound with steel chains. Hurrying footsteps still follow me and their muffled echoes drum in my ears. Each morning when I awake, my eyes gather the threads of sunlight from my bed and I jump up, trying to convince myself that a new day is about to begin and the damned footsteps will stop coming after me. I examine the wild rose growing by the entrance and give it a drop of water. But there are light footsteps thudding against my eardrums and my heart as I step out on to the black, uneven pavement. I pretend to be indifferent and then a deep feeling of gloom wells up in me, spreading to the ends of my fingers and cutting deep furrows in me. I console myself by looking at the stonework of the walls on either side of me as I go along, and breathe in the morning air, pure with the scent of trees, and feel my annoyance and my sense of being surrounded lift from me. I pass the sweetseller's stall and buy a sweet pastry and eat it as I walk, my heels rapping the asphalt. I only wish that I could make them realise that I'm free, free, in spite of them following me, the sound of their shoes, their reports on me, free despite everything.'

7

Spring hung frivolous goblets with fine, wine-coloured threads inside them on the pomegranate tree. The sun laughed in the streets and I saw Adel walking with his friends. I found myself pulled towards the greenness which poured into his eyes in the spring light. Samar had talked to us about her cousin Adel, how steady he was and how hard he worked at his studies; he was gifted at maths, that heavy subject which gave me indigestion whenever I had to do it. He loved Nasser and, in spite of the regulations which the secret police in our area had imposed, had his photograph stuck inside his wardrobe where the informers wouldn't see it, and he listened to certain radio broadcasts, an activity punishable in Jericho by imprisonment or constant harassment and intimidation.

It was love sprung from stories and novels, the gentle sweet emotion depicted on those furtively read pages, which I and the other girls discussed in awed tones with agitation clutching at our hearts, or studied as it appeared with magical flashes on the faces of cinema heroines when their eyes sparkled in expressions of wild joy.

I felt . . . I saw the grass green of his eyes every time I passed close to him and gazed delightedly at him. I was seized by an obscure craving to find out what I didn't know and I searched through the works of the ancient desert poets to find the verses about passion exploding in their blood. When I saw him by chance birds of paradise spread their wings in my blood, and shot up into the sky above the city making a rainbow which fluttered between us when we walked in the same street. I pictured us crouching at either end of the coloured rainbow extending between us and knew that it was in this street he would be forced to find out that I existed, and I would be driven to scale impossible heights to reach the fine mist of dreams released in me when I saw him.

I began going to Samar's house on the pretext of doing some studying with her, confident that I would meet him there by chance. When the day came, I cast my eyes down into my lap pretending to be unmoved, then occupied myself by looking around at the family's antique chairs, at the photographs of their forebears in large black frames, and at the gold-rimmed teacups inside a glass-fronted cupboard where a mirror reflected the images of its precious contents. The difference between their houses and ours seemed enormous, but I didn't care; I even grew bold enough to ask him a short way of working out arithmetical progressions.

On that night in June 1967 we crowded on to the staircase in the entrance to the old brick building. Aircraft made a hellish din in the violet skies above Jericho and flares streaked across the dark night like rockets on a film set.

What we felt wasn't terror; it was amazement, shock, unpreparedness. We hadn't yet realised the enormity of what was happening.

Tanks adorned with the branches of trees moved up to the front lines. The people lined up at the roadside, applauding with delirious joy. God is great. And the balconies, brimming with salutations and cheers of delighted encouragement, rang to the same cry.

That evening we sat on the ground, our patience nearly at an end as exasperation, boredom and fading conviction got the better of us. We could hear the distant thunder of night-flying aircraft at regular intervals, and see flare bombs spread out over the purple sheet of night like lamps on ships at sea. Without surprise, we heard the tanks' squeaking chains as they retreated to the other side of the river. They were going to refit them, so the battle must be hard and fierce, the inhabitants of the building reassured one another. I had a pain in my back and the smooth edges of the stone stairs dug into me. Only the civil defence volunteers followed their instructions with obvious relish: there was a frenzied blaring of sirens each time a light showed, or the flicker of a candle.

I grew tired of the gloomy darkness and the dumb sitting on the staircase crowded with others come like me to shelter, and went up to the house, holding Sima's soft hand as she stumbled against the edges of furniture and into passageways. She moved in close to me and I encircled her with an arm grown stiff from the miserable time spent on the staircase. I sat glumly in the dark and stared at the blankets I'd so eagerly fixed to the windows. I failed to understand who this person might be whom we credited with the power to do something significant to our home.

All day there had been dancing and congratulations exchanged and drinks offered each time an enemy aircraft was destroyed. It was a wedding atmosphere, no less, and like a wedding it rang with unarticulated hopes and desires; as the numbers went up we'd drink to these new, intense emotions. In the gloom I felt a box of sweets left open on the table; it had lain there all day long and the flies had raided it merrily without us paying any attention to them.

I felt drowsiness creeping over me, a bird of prey plucking out all my wakefulness with its bulging talons. I was about to let go and drift into sleep when a heavy, prolonged knocking sounded on the front door, echoing down the hall and through the house, hoarse and scared. I had to light a candle to see my way, while the hammering fists opened out and beat against the door with all ten fingers. My father got out of bed hurriedly, and I went down the hall carrying the candle. 'Who is it?' I called.

'Salima Al-Hajja,' she shouted at the top of her voice. 'Hurry up, God protect you!'

'Just a minute,' I answered her, apprehension stubbornly accumulating in my throat.

The knocking grew louder as she pounded the door in a frenzy. My father fumbled with the key in the lock, searching for his torch. Salima Al-Hajja rushed into the hall, roaring like a wounded lioness, 'Tell your father to get the doctor who lives next door to you straight away. I've got them with me in the car. We were hit by planes this afternoon on the road near Al-Azariyya. They were wounded and the girl's legs are badly hurt.'

Amer hadn't been hit. His brother Saber was wounded and Saber's daughter had lacerations on her thighs, which the doctor dressed expertly. Muffled in her stained outer robe, Salima Al-Hajja dried her tears, but then she broke into wails of lamentation: what nice man was going to believe that one of the casualties of the attack had been her granddaughter's virginity?

8

From the first, second and fourth chapters of the elegies of Aramaea:

> 'From the sound of the horseman and the archer all the city is fleeing. The people have gone into the forests and climbed up on the rocks. All the cities are abandoned and there is no living being in them. And you, O ruined one, what are you doing? You dress in scarlet, deck yourself in gold, make up your eyes with antimony, but this beautifying of yourself is in vain for your lovers have rejected you. They are asking for your life.'

The lamentations of the past rose up from the Old Testament as I turned the yellow pages. Different wars across history but the sensations in defeat were always the same. Had it been a defeat? I doubted it. They presented it to us in this guise to complement their own defeat of three years before. The women and old people congregated like flocks of pelicans in their long, snowy headcovers and the men began to stream forward on the long road that began at the city gates and ended in the pine forests. Warm farewells were exchanged and packages of food and bags of fruit bestowed on the dirt pavement in front of the monument to the Unknown Soldier in Ashrafiya in Amman. Bullets whistled by, and the young men drew their guns as they boarded trucks loaded with weapons which no longer worked.

It was a choice between another terrible month like this September or your exodus into the woods and hills. The rifles bowed their heads and exploded among the rocks and scree and wild plants. The trucks moved away and a long anguished blaze of shots rose into the sky, releasing the pent-up goodbyes; it pealed out, expressing unforgettable sorrow and defeat. Salima Al-Hajja wept, and the sorrowing peal went on sounding inside me, uprooting and sweeping away the ebb and flow of the tides, the compass for the maps and the land of faded dreams. The seagulls cried harshly, hovering above the restless waves, and the women wept in their embroidered dresses whose threads had worn away under the rays of a blazing sun which spread its scorching heat stickily over everything. The fighters set off for the chilly heights of the forests, leaving behind them empty brass shell cases, a scattering of little stones from the wheels of their vehicles, a monument to the Unknown Soldier - which means corpses too numerous to count - and bagpipe music from a military band broadcast by Jordanian Radio.

'The battle has begun.'

His tone was quite neutral as he picked up his gun and ammunition. A cold shudder ran through me and left me bleak and desolate. He was off to join his position; but where could I go? Where would I be of any use? My basic training in loading and unloading a gun didn't amount to much; my skills were theoretical and I had no previous experience of the battlefield. When Jericho fell I hadn't been there. The city had tumbled into the abyss at the beginning of summer, and now at the end of another summer the trenches of September had appeared. This time I had everything except experience and experience was galloping towards me in a cloud of dust on the back of a horse as swift as lightning discharging showers of molten metal as it tore along.

The noise, the noise. Like a huge boiler exploding, the bubbles of lead revolving madly then falling like rocks from the savage mangonels of the Tartar armies. The sound of the five hundred millimetre cannon going off: it ripped and burned through the air, sounding as if it exploded twice, once when it was fired and again when it hit its target.

It's experience, just experience, I would say to myself.

Then a huge mill grinding rock, all the quarries in the high mountains exploding in pieces. Another rumbling sound pierced the first with steel and jagged tongues of fire. This was reassuring: the Dushka anti-aircraft guns were still in position.

Shells came from every direction, whistling and roaring and shuddering through the hot air, and the battle was on.

(What had been surprising in 1967 was the timing; the deafening noise like all the din and chaos of hell sliding down through the atmosphere; the sunlight shining on the wings of the enemy aircraft, then boring into my back as I lay face down on the dried-up dusty bed of a rivulet; the vehicles coming to a halt at a top of a slope as we rushed down it. And now that noise and conflagration was happening on a road in Amman.)

I didn't know what to do. He took his weapon and went away and a cold shudder trembled in my veins and left me bleak and desolate. So I sat feeding my bewilderment and my powerful sense that the world had shrunk into a little patch of darkness flowing down over my toes and spilling into my palms which I had clasped firmly together in agitation. The hands of the clock moved forward very slowly.

(I knew nothing of the world but the high thin note of the monotonous martial music issuing from the open doors of the empty cars, our bagpipes mingling with the roar of the cruel aeroplanes as they attacked. I saw thousands of feet hurrying over the asphalt, running helplessly along the side of the road in the direction of the bridge.

The feet kept coming, thousands of them lifted off the ground, put down, lifted up again. A car swerved, letting out a harsh squeal, and continued moving over the earth at the side of the road. On the asphalt the body of a woman lay stiff and motionless in a black peasant dress. The black of her hair mingled with the black of the asphalt and the black of her dress. Only her feet showed, cracked and hard like the hooves of a goat. Nobody turned to look at her. Nobody seemed to see her. People jostled one another and surged forward bearing children and baggage on their shoulders and fleeing from the tongues of fire spilling out of the sky. The horizon had disappeared behind the hurrying regular movement of the feet, and the shabby dull clothes had blended with the curves of the hills all around. The melancholy sun oozed heat and sweat in tears which rolled in big drops down the indistinguishable faces.

There was a flash of sunlight reflected off aircraft wings and the crowd scattered or threw themselves down at the side of the road, shaking in terror at the black swallows which descended for a moment over a section of the hurrying throng, poured fire over them, then soared back into the skies.

On this bleak road, all wasteland and hills, I gathered up my longing for Jericho and burnt it without regret. I knew very well that we would never return. I'd rushed all round our house, confused and upset, and they'd shouted at me, 'Quickly! All you need is nightclothes. In two or three days we'll be back.'

I felt sickened, thinking that this story of coming back in a couple of days was a pathetic re-enactment of what we'd always heard from those who'd left in the first disaster in 1948. 'Two or three days,' they said. 'Until the situation improves.'

For the Jews had come in all over the West Bank and only Jericho was left ahead of them.

They took their little doorkeys with them just as my grandfather had taken his big metal key before them, and we departed. They took nightclothes and two bars of soap and I left Kanafani's book *The Land of the Sad Orange* open by chance on the table.

Out on the bleak road I said goodbye to Jericho for a long time. I left the hot summers and the breezes which blew at the end of them, giving off sweet smells of harvesting and threshing, the mild winters and the puddles of rain where the clouds danced, the big smooth stones paving the pathways in the vast citrus groves. In our school was a wall newspaper, its title adorned with coloured drawings of flowers, and in amongst its letters we'd secretly drawn a little Palestinian flag. From here I couldn't see the dark purple of Mount Qarantal, full of a mystery and splendour which dominated the houses and army camps built on its slopes. No longer would I be able to breathe in the smell of milk mixed with the black sheep's wool, a pungent acrid aroma which accumulated in the air when the warm white liquid was boiled, and stimulated our appetites. If we swallowed some of the milk from our bowls and arrived home with less than we should have had, our mothers put it down to the vendor selling us short. Nor would I be able to watch the people flocking, anxious and hesitant, to the doctor's clinic next door, and leaving a little later with some reassurance decanted into bottles of free medicine.

There would be no songs, those long Eastern songs pouring out into the night over the street lamps by whose pale light the secondary schoolboys studied and sent secret passionate glances to girls standing on balconies. No longer would we live in a house near the Greek Orthodox Church with its monks whose long hair was tied up in buns under little black caps, and its ceremonies ablaze with incense and ancient organ music sighing through the stained glass windows.

The dew would gather in transparent balloons on the stems of the wild mint whose thick roots plunged down into the irrigation ditches. And I was going away from the mint and from the stones of Qarantal and the broad banana leaves, away from the destinies of everyone I knew. They had set out in different directions on a crisscrossing network of paths, making a puzzle it was difficult to solve. I remembered Thurayya trembling as she drank the citrus juice, or mulberry syrup, that her father sold in his shop, while the green olives went trembling down into the casks unripe, gentle, sour, to be immersed in salt.

The bombardment produced a dense tangle of injury and pale iron death while the shells echoed with fierce insolence over the roof of the stone house. I had to find my place in the songs of thunder that raged over the mountain slopes of Amman.

9

We were sitting in our café in the country. The branches of the vine, brown inclining to black, were bare except for a few leaves here and there. 'Why do you love me, Shaher?' I asked him on a sudden impulse. 'It's an odd question, isn't it? But there are things going round in my head like motes of dust in the slipstream of a revolving fan. There's a long discussion going on inside me, another girl there talking to me, day and night. Is this just another fiction I'm making use of to avoid facing up to reality and to escape from the legendary evils of the world, which terrify me so much? Or does the faith I have in our relationship mean a sudden opening up of my consciousness? And how will I know if you're really different from the ones I've known before you?'

To myself I said, 'Is this love?'

The shock of pleasure and creativity, then the shifting sands which end in emptiness. Is this the explosive tenderness which becomes love in time, and not simply a desire to possess another person? Is it new photographs which I'll put in my album then tear out, hating even to touch them?

I stopped asking myself these questions and waited agitatedly. He frowned. 'I'm probably like them in a lot of ways,' he said, 'but you'll have to find out for yourself.'

He chewed on a twig, and continued slowly, 'I love you. But I might not be right for you. You don't own me. You won't always be able to find me. You'll search for me along muddy roads and lonely pathways and they'll tell you, "He was here five minutes ago, but he's gone." And they'll say that wherever you go, and I'll be on my way back to the dry leaves and the smell of guns and metal. And perhaps a voice inside me will urge me again and again to cling to your warmth that spreads around me and engulfs the dawn stars I watch over. But I won't do it. Is it egocentric to expose myself to you, then ask you to love me? The things that I know are deep inside you tempt me to be foolhardy; the clusters of lights in your face, fragrant with joy; your ringing laughter which sounds somehow like crying; your enthusiasm and sincerity at times when some girls would insult me by putting on an act, lying, flattering. You bury your nails deep in the mud but it doesn't suck you under, however dirty it makes you. You're not like the sultans' slave girls who pretended to be pure and unsullied.

'You ask me why I come to see you, why I stay with you when you're distraught like this. I'm not Christ, or a social reformer, and I'm not that decorated young god whom others like to see as a noble saint. But there are people in the world who feel happy when they go back to being as they were when they started out, and with you I stop feeling the falseness which is in people's faces and bodies. I see you as you are, taking my lost love in and shutting out the night.'

My voice was dry, its fire extinguished, and it seemed to move apart from me, a sound on its own: 'Why does love always have to be portrayed in crazy stories where people are made to look ridiculous and spend their time leaping over fictitious walls, while the obstacles which really exist are ignored? They made me hate the whole idea of love. I saw it as a horrible form of torture, a series of shocks to the system, a kind of slow death like someone throwing himself off the roof of a skyscraper, waiting second by second for his head to shatter on the ground, wondering when he'll become a mangled heap of flesh streaming blood, and when this dizziness and dreadful empty space will end and how long it will be before everything's over for good.'

'Who told you that love had to have a trademark with a certain name on it and anything else was a fraud?' remarked Shaher calmly. ' "Beware of imitations", as it says on Nablus soap. I might be like them in a lot of ways, and I might say things to you that other people have said before me. It doesn't matter. I'm not going to say that I'm not or I won't. You're the one who has to find that out. But with you I go back to how I was when I started and forget every lesson I learnt in the past from other girls. I begin with you, not from where I left off with the others, but from the point at which I was a child in my whims and emotions. Personal choices. Are you convinced by the notion of personal choices?'

The lost streets of Jericho are redolent with the scent of many trees. Red buds grow and blossom throughout the four seasons. Jericho glows in the light of thousands of tropical suns flaring in my blood, beginning their never-ending cycle in my heart. I wasn't Archimedes, so I couldn't shout his famous 'Eureka!', but I'd found a friend at a time when to be good was to be hard, in the womb of changing days. The weather was springlike, ash-coloured and imperfect like the severed bridges. The citrus groves of Jericho were ablaze with fragrant lemons and the choking smell of gunpowder.

Plain words, obscure words, what do they do? He was talking to me, 'We'll stay together, Jinan.'

I didn't answer. I stared at a little ant hurrying over the ground with a piece of yellow straw and heard him continuing, 'How would your family react?'

I'd been wondering the same thing myself. 'I don't know, I haven't had to raise the subject with them before.'

The ant dropped its straw and began circling it as he spoke again: 'It's simple. Tell them that you've met a person who suits you and that you get on well together and understand one another emotionally and intellectually. They need clichés to reassure them and make them agree.'

We laughed uproariously together. Why do I love your laughter as much as I do? Why does your face look like the face of a saint and a pagan idol at the same time?

'They'll say, my dear sir, that they don't like poor people, even though they were poor themselves once. My paternal aunts and my maternal aunts will complain loudly at my stupidity. An educated girl like you going after a poor man who's committed to a way of life that we're trying to get our children away from. What about the sacrifices we made to turn you into a steady, sensible girl? And now you want to become a tramp and live a life where you'll be constantly under threat, and have no security . . .'

Laughter dominated the rest of our conversation and we didn't bother to discuss the subject any further. For many things had been dislodged from their places in the previous order of our lives and certainty was a new equation which we could solve only by working with total dedication and immersing ourselves in experience. An astonishing, exciting reality had taken shape in our path, so we had begun to look to it to make decisions for us, and to take our answers from its mouth.

10

He was looking out of the door of the aircraft, a rounded door leading to the metal flight of steps propped against it. The muzzle of his pistol was pointed at the chest of one of the hostages. How slight and fragile he seemed, to be in charge of a jumbo jet. Was this Amer to whom I'd willingly given over my childhood as we played in the town squares and climbed the sycamore tree? Hands up! And I would raise my hands in abject surrender, the cowboy's prisoner. I would chase him with bare feet and forget where I'd left my shoes when it was time to go home. We used to sit on an abandoned millstone and I made the round hole at the centre into a store for the broken biscuits and bits of cheese we smuggled from home. Amer stopped paying attention to me when his friends came and they played their games of guns and chasing and forgot about me. I could always expect a sound beating when I went back home and my mother would scream in my face, 'You tomboy! When will you become more responsible and stop acting like a boy? The girl next door is your age and she does all the washing up for her mother and cleans the house.'

I've had short hair since I was a child. I was angry when they first cut it off but my mother didn't heed my protestations. 'Your hair's not straight, girl. It takes ages to do in the morning. The boyish cut suits you better.'

And when I was a bit older they would flatter me, saying, 'Suleyman Bey's wife has her daughter's hair cut *à la garçon.*'

Where are you, Amer? I remember how you used to wink when our parents were telling us off. Our bottled-up laughter would erupt and our punishment would be all the harsher. I was crouching in the garden one day, constructing a house of flat stones and decorating it with flowers. You arrived all at once and destroyed it with a powerful kick from your big flat foot. I cried and cried, pulling your hair and striking you with both hands, screaming at you in street language that I would never have dared to use in front of my family. And you laughed and laughed, and then stood there smiling as if nothing had happened. You were the mean one who put smudges of black ink all over my exercise books when I got higher marks than you at school, and divulged the secrets of my first love to the youths of the neighbourhood. You showed them the boy who followed me on his bicycle when I came out of school in the afternoon, with my case under my arm full of books we weren't allowed to read. The shouts and mocking remarks continued to fly whenever the bicycle and its rider came into view: I wouldn't have been able to forgive anyone but Amer.

Amer. The colour of the sea and the smell of forgotten desires. In his debate with me, he used to say, 'Civilisation's a whore between the thighs of history, and she switches around from nation to nation, and continent to continent. Why the hell did the Arabs emerge from their encounter with civilisation without so much as a camel?'

Amer let the deadline pass. The armoured vehicles of the security forces and the airport control towers with their radios, and even the passengers sitting in the seats on the aircraft which he commanded, all conspired against him. Nothing had happened up till now, but I knew exactly what was going to happen. It was just a matter of time. Amer: childhood drawing a knife to protect itself, and lashing out with it, stabbing the face of the world. Your victims will snatch the knife away from you and the red lights of the trucks will bear down on you and they'll fire at you and you'll fire at them until time is extinguished . . . the time of the civilisation which you're trying to find. Aircraft, aircraft and more aircraft. And what then? Do you think you're doing away with a bit of history's whorishness, say the bit between her heels and toes? You're surrounded at this minute by hundreds and thousands of commercial aircraft with innocents like you on board. Salima Al-Hajja must be dumbstruck as she listens to the foreign news bulletins talking about her youngest son as a terrorist and a murderer. She'll gather earth and ashes and rub them all over her face. In their eyes you're the executioner, but what you really are is the sacrificial ram. Once you said quite calmly, 'The external operations need more precision and people with steadier nerves.'

My heart was sore when I heard that; I knew before they did what you were thinking about, realised before them that you didn't say a thing in that cool, calm way without acting on it. O childhood, lost on the curve of a blade which will finish off you and them. Will this moment be wiped away out of sight of time so that I'll be able to see you standing in front of me again, alive, whole, real? Will you come back, Amer?

Long days later, days I spent roaming the Bab Khan Al-Zait Market alleyway by alleyway and resting under the ancient stone archways of Old Jerusalem, my father came back to us, fully expecting to be put in prison again. We returned to Jericho, but not to our old house in Sabiha Street; rents were lower near the graveyard. We rented a house with latticed wooden windows entwined with climbing plants, a front garden where we grew lettuce and mint, and big cages for rearing pigeons and other birds. Every morning I would go to see them and teach my songs to my new feathered pupils. I would yell at them to stop their cheeping and cooing, but only the little chicks heard me. In the afternoon I would rush out to the square to join the crowd of boys and girls and play hopscotch. We drew big squares with our fingers in the soft earth and hopped over them, not heeding the graveyard watchman who threatened us with tales about a horned yellow snake: a huge snake, ten metres long, with insides big enough to accommodate a whole child each time the sacred nature of the graveyard wasn't respected. We were scared of it really, but our attention was concentrated on the stone one of us was pushing along with one foot, taking care not to let it touch any lines. We heard the rattle of tambourines and the thumps of big drums and stopped our game, waiting to see the joyful procession go by: the only drums to be heard in the streets of Jericho were those gracing wedding festivities. In the distance a group of townspeople appeared, men and women, dressed in long black clothes. They moved slowly and sedately carrying a box, a narrow, elongated box, draped in green cloth. At their head walked a man in a white turban with a big drum slung around his waist, which he beat with a little stick. The people sobbed as they went along, carrying green flags adorned with writing and pictures of crossed swords. One of the boys cried, 'Run away! It's a funeral.' And they all ran off, wailing and yelling, fleeing from the funeral procession. I didn't understand, and stood rooted to the spot; the mysterious, ugly thing passed by, and I was left there alone.

11

Blood ran over the floor of the clinic. It congealed, colouring the tiles deep crimson. First there was a trembling which attacked the walls, the chairs and the one table loaded down with bottles of blood and antiseptic, then a huge explosion in the doorway of the house, dislodging dense layers of compressed air and pushing them inside, and the sudden flash of blue-grey-white light before our eyes. 'When a bomb lands that near you, you can't help feeling shocked,' said the nurse afterwards.

The bottles fell over, slid along the table and crashed to the ground in a sudden rush. There was consternation among the casualties lying on blankets and some of them tried unsuccessfully to move. In the midst of their restless stirrings an anguished scream ran out and hysterical wailing rose up from the tin-roofed shack next door. Shock spread over the pale listless faces, and one of the female first-aid workers rushed out, crying to the others to follow her.

Just a short while before I'd been making my way, armed, to the centre, slipping through the alleyways with a group of fighters. The tank had been crouching there like a huge metal prehistoric animal, its hatch a great ogre's eye, glinting repulsively with power and arrogance. A dinosaur? No, the age of dinosaurs was long past. With the rest of the group I took cover in the entrance to the alley and we made ready to cross it. The tank blocked the other end leading into the main street, and the muzzles of snipers' rifles moved on the roof of the Jabal Al-Hussein cinema. 'Ready!' they said.

I moved the hammer back ready to put a bullet in the firing chamber but the movement merely passed through my trembling fingers while the hammer remained stubbornly still in my hand. A chill crept over my limbs. The tank might rush towards us as we went across the exposed area between us and them. They'd climb down from it and I'd be powerless to fire this damned bullet. Could my weapon really be out of action in such a humiliating and unreasonable way? 'Ready!' they said, and we crossed at a run, watching out for the tank and its crew. One of my companions examined my weapon and found a bullet already in the chamber. 'You didn't need another one. That was why it wouldn't go in,' he said. 'It'll be all right next time. Make sure you have a good look in the chamber.'

I wasn't interested in the technical details. The important thing was that we were across, for what was certain was that every little open space in the camp was now within range of the mortar and howitzer shells.

They came through the door of the first-aid centre carrying the wounded; the bomb still reverberated noisily and fragments of it preceded them. The little girl made an inhuman noise, like the growling of a lioness fatally wounded. The nurse leapt over to the unconscious woman: her legs were shattered, a mangled bloody mess of torn muscles and bones protruding through burnt flesh. Her daughter gave a long despairing cry of 'Mummy! Mummy!' and her small trembling body turned the dark yellow of turmeric. A shudder passed over the woman's waxen immobile face; her features were dissolving away. The girl's mouth went rigid, then she exhaled and let out several long, frightened cries. We tore her dress and uncovered a deep conical wound on her small chest; the blood gushed from it incessantly and gathered on the floor at her feet in a venomous crimson pool.

There was only basic primitive equipment in the place, and her devasting panic-stricken screams of 'Mummy . . . Mummy,' dominated everything. The eyes of the wounded were focused intently, with faint hopefulness, on the nurse as he began to stitch the wounds. Could a needle halt a plunging torrent? There was nothing to inject against blood poisoning: deliverance was a mysterious amulet administered by crazy fate to the gaping inflamed wounds. Day departed as if by magic, spirited away by a charm, like a horseman whom nothing could stop on his flight from the seven hills of Amman.

12

When I awoke in the early dawn, I missed the cooing of the pigeons and the noise of the smaller birds fighting and the neighbour's mangy dog barking. A stranger was carrying me in his arms and I was wrapped in an unfamiliar thick blanket. My mother carried my little sister, with her head poking out like an orange. The clatter of a dusty horse's hooves rose from the rocks around us, melodious, echoing, noisy in the quiet of the vast silent countryside. They wouldn't let me ride the horse, saying that it had a lot of baggage to carry, so I walked along with them in silence, watching its feet as they slithered over rocks and down steep inclines. We reached a cave lit by a small paraffin lamp; it was as big as a proper house although it had dark gloomy corners. When the mats and blankets were spread on the ground I recaptured the sleep I'd lost among the rocks and hills.

In the morning it was magnificent: open countryside with outcrops of grey rock, wild carnations and beautiful sun. There I might play as I pleased with no scolding, no orders. I wouldn't have to wake up in the morning to go to school, where we just copied the same lesson over and over again until we were tired of it. Here no one would dare ask me if I knew how to write 'cinnamon' without hesitating or making a mistake. I wondered who the good people were who had brought us here and provided us with delicious fresh food and torches and spare batteries, treating us like a mother spoiling her daughter. I heard them talking about running away from the king's cavalry in the Hebron mountains, but wasn't able to appreciate the seriousness of this new game. With their children I amused myself eating roast chickpeas and freshly baked bread. Then I heard my mother asking my father, 'Will we have to move to Doura tomorrow?'

'Yes. There's a battalion surrounding the area and they might find us if we stay here.'

In Doura, a small village nearby, I got to know the mud-brick houses of the countryside with strings of onions stored in cavities in the walls, and the peasant women's black dresses glowing with brilliant festive colours. My mother wore one of their embroidered dresses and it made her look more beautiful. I asked them for one like hers and they gave me a long green dress gathered at the waist. I was delighted when I discovered the freedom it provided for jumping, skipping and running through the fields. Green grasshoppers chirped in tune with our babbling voices and alighted on our fingers, then, without troubling to make our acquaintance, flew off like us through the peach orchards and among the branches of the low trees overhanging the irrigation ditch. We wandered over the broad land and by streams and rivers, only returning in the evening with the flocks. Three-cornered bells hung around the animals' necks, ringing sweetly like spoons stirring sugar in glasses of mint tea. The sound of their feet, quiet and solid, came to my ears when the barn door was opened, as their round hooves moved slowly and softly on the moist rich earth.

The smell of dried blood rose in the air, mingling with other smells of wounds and antiseptic. Water stopped dripping out of the rusty tap, and we could no longer treat all the patients in the onslaught of attacks which occurred every few minutes. On the eighth or ninth day of the battle scores of the dead were splattered by the bodies of insects which had lost their way in the blind alleys between the corpses. In the end the UNWRA school in the camp was filled with the bloody legs and faces of the wounded, and the mosque became a place of assembly for the dead who were brought in furtively while the heavy shelling was in progress. Those who carried them in at a run averted their eyes from the threadbare sheets which hid their rags, taking cover from the snipers behind the low walls of the buildings made of wood and sheets of metal which housed the shops.

I was touched, but also embarrassed and surprised, when a housewife in one of the one-roomed shacks insisted on going to the communal kitchen to make coffee, bitter coffee, ground with smoke from the bombs. I heard her repeating fearful prayers, then she raised her voice as if to encourage herself, as she cursed the devils who'd caused these disasters. 'Those soldiers with their long braids and the gun barrels on their tanks want nothing less than to destroy the city completely,' she said. 'I swear they're not human.'

As a bomb passed over the house, she shrieked an accompaniment to its long, piercing whine; she was a hospitable woman who would defy the whistle of bombs to make a cup of coffee, and my suppressed anguish exploded in me as I watched her doggedly standing in the roofless kitchen, and I remembered my daily tours around the camp.

'Auntie, your children are grown up, and I'm sure you'd like to learn how to write their names and help them with their studies.'

'Me, daughter? Read and write?'

'What's wrong with that, Auntie? Things have changed a bit now for you. The children are older and you have fewer responsibilities than before. We hold knitting classes in the Women's Centre too if you'd like to come along.'

'All that's way beyond me. And what would the neighbours say? "An old thing like her going to primary school." No, it's not even worth discussing. I'll soon be dead anyway.'

Then, angrily and sorrowfully, she told me the story of Umm Khaled's quarrel with her grown-up son, who'd seen her going to the Women's Centre with paper and a pen: 'Why don't you come and learn how to handle a Simonov, Mother?'

No answer.

'But you were enthusiastic last time when you learnt about Kalashnikovs, and you told us that arms were the thing we must have to defeat our enemies.'

I remembered another woman's story. 'My fiancé Jasem was visiting us,' she'd told me, 'and he didn't want me to leave him to go to the Centre. "They say that arms are an ornament for a man," he said to me, "but they have never been an ornament for a woman."

'Then he got angry and shouted at me, "Sit down, you useless bitch. Who put such ideas into your head?"

"At the time of the first disaster," I answered him, "I mean when we lost Palestine, we didn't have arms and we didn't have the right policy for the people. Now the times and the circumstances are different.''

''To hear you speaking,'' he countered angrily, ''anyone would think that there was no place for men in the world any more. If I or your brother or the man next door carries arms, that's something to be proud of, but they'd only be any use to you and the other girls to wave in each other's faces. Calm down and start thinking straight.''

'He swore that he'd break off the engagement if I went out and left him,' finished the woman.

13

We had to run away. A cavalry unit combed the area; drizzle fell on the rounded tops of their heavy steel helmets, and their whips cracked in the muddy, steamy air. Nobody from Doura told them anything. They all said, 'We don't know anything, nor do the peach trees nor the mewing cats nor the grasshoppers in the green fields.'

They took me and Sima to Salima Al-Hajja's house in Jerusalem by ourselves without my mother or father. My father was arrested at the border post as he was trying to leave, but my mother managed to escape with the baby daughter she was breastfeeding. She disguised herself in the old-fashioned black headgear which Salima Al-Hajja wore, put a transparent veil over her face and took off her wedding ring.

For two months Salima Al-Hajja ran from one police station to another, trying to get identity papers for us so that she could send us to our mother. I heard her repeating to herself the slogans the women of Jerusalem shouted when they went out on demonstrations, and the tears glistened on her face, and on her eyelashes which had a dusting of flour on them when she made the flat circles of dough and stacked them in the tray, ready to be sent to the baker. Then in a dejected whisper, barely audible, she began repeating dully and bitterly, 'Bread, peace and freedom', and, echoing her own words, 'Bread, solace and freedom', remembering Salwa which means 'solace' in Arabic, a friend of my mother's who'd left in an earlier exodus.

She talked to the neighbours a lot.

'Where are their mother and father?'

'They're communists and nationalists. Oh, the miseries of prison and exile!'

What else? Nothing. There I was walking about in the courtyard which was paved with big, smooth stones, trying to dig up the moss growing in the cracks between them, and finding life hard to bear. So I didn't listen to what the grown ups said, and I went out and wandered through the crisscrossing alleyways until I came to the Church of the Resurrection and the Mosque of Umar the Just. I went through a little door, almost like a hole in the wall, and into the church, and there I beheld the sad, silent Virgin, and watched the drops of oil running down the sides of the illuminated statues. When I'd drunk in the heady perfume of the incense I went out, and on my way home I went by the big flight of steps carved in the rock leading to Umar's Mosque and jumped up and down them if nobody told me to stop. But when I reached home I was always given a beating as a punishment for my improper behaviour.

When I went with Amer to the communal oven to fetch the bread, he told one of the boys from school all about me and my sister. I felt miserable, and as we went along I demanded angrily, 'How could you tell him? He might be a spy or a policeman's son for all we know.'

14

I felt slightly dizzy and wondered to myself if the world was spinning round faster these days. I'm Jinan, the girl who used to dream of being reincarnated as a boy and making up for all the things I'd missed out on in childhood and adolescence: going out around the town at any hour without a member of my family to escort me; ambling along the dusty paths among the orchards without someone to watch over me; studying on summer nights by the light of the streetlamps like the boys did; going around with whomever I wanted without my family interfering and choosing for me. As it was I had the strong sensation that I was like a chicken, raised for an obvious, clearly defined economic purpose. From home to school and back again I went, acquiring the features of the most superior type of education and upbringing in the eyes of the world. In time my progress would be reversed and marriage would be my lot, as they say; then for a change I would move from my husband's room to the kitchen, and from the kitchen to the children's rooms and the guest rooms.

I was an intelligent girl and I knew all the things that were likely to happen if a strange man came to our house prompted by a desire for friendship or affection. So I understood that I was supposed to fall in love while forbidden to use my five senses. But then I fell in love with Adel, and I made a conscious effort to open up every pore of my body in response to the calls which seemed to come at me from the four corners of the world; to understand, to know, to see, to smell, to feel, taste, interpret and analyse, and to accept or refuse according to what I myself wanted.

Adel didn't really see me at first, then he began to notice the fire on my cheeks when I talked to him, the sun blazing in my face when he looked in my direction. On the whole I was too young and unimportant to arouse his full attention: he was Adel, son of a proud, old-established family. For his sake I wore high heels and gave up biting my nails, and painted them a nice shiny colour. I emptied my bag of the books by Sartre forbidden by our school, the poems of Jamal Buthaina, the philosophy of Heraclitus, and learnt to consult magazines to find out the latest fashions. Adel wanted me fresh and shining bright like a basket of ripe strawberries with not a rotten one among them, and I loved him more than my books and my friends and the monotonous babble of my teachers. But he never let me forget that he was the more important, the more upper class, the more powerful of the two of us, and that I was still foolish and hadn't mastered the art of joining automatically in the game of cat and mouse.

One day I came to him in the noonday heat, and announced to him that he was free of his naive lover, who'd loved him without experience or knowledge, and she was free of the humiliation of melting before him like a silver sugar crystal from a rich family's sugar bowl.

As Thurayya and I came down the steps of the lecture room we heard powerful waves of sound rolling across the brilliant morning air. She smiled, and said humorously, 'The enemy aircraft are crossing our skies.'

The next moment bombs rained down on a guerrilla base near the college. God, this was the second time. We ran and threw ourselves down at the foot of a peach tree where the ground had been hollowed out by a previous explosion. The echoing waves of sound collided and raged over the earth, and clouds of dust and stones were strewn about and fell among the dried-up ends of roots protruding from the sides of the small crater. Pieces of metal like black swastikas blazed in the sky, shuddering and swooping to earth in sudden spiralling dives. The brilliant red of my dress began to make me uneasy. Fear hovered on the surface of the solid, leaden sky, and in my scared fantasy it became a bullet which described a vertical trajectory and entered my spine, opening up a narrow channel in it. Cautiously and with some difficulty, I picked up my exercise books and textbooks and placed them along my back one behind the other; they made a gentle cover to deflect the heat which had started to flood along my spine.

Thurayya was lying beside me and her heartbeats were audible, jumping in time to the shuddering of the tree roots round about us. I thought then how all the world powers had been incapable of halting this sudden damned bombing raid. Thurayya reached up her hand and touched the charm on a golden chain around her neck which her mother had given her. I thought of calling out for my mother but she was dead, I told myself, lying in a tomb sealed with a white marble stone while we lay in an open tomb under a grey sky humming with silver swastikas which turned black in the shadow of the clouds. Volubly I cursed all little bomb craters, leaden skies, inexhaustible tanks of aircraft fuel.

The planes went away after several hours, or years, or minutes. Branches hung broken where they had been hit by machine-gun fire from the air. Car horns blared in alarm and confusion, and vehicles collided on the main road. Swarms of students searched the cypresses and pines for burning tree trunks. We climbed up out of the crater and brushed the earth and dust and leaves from our clothes. There was only the length of the road between me and him. I went to him and said, 'I love you, Shaher,' and sat with him in his empty house on the drab worn blankets spread on the floor of his empty room. 'Tomorrow I'll bring a teapot and some coffee,' I told him.

He'd moved there recently. He bent low before me like a deposed monarch and waved an arm. 'These vast white walls are at your disposal. Write whatever you want on them.' I wrote, 'Love is a bourgeois deviation. I fell in love and I wanted to be grown up. But when I grew up I lost the joys of childhood and gained the sorrows of age.'

He took the long chalk from me and broke it in half. With one half he wrote, 'Have you lost the world and gained your soul?' and with the other, 'But since you aren't Rome, I can't burn you.'

I wrote my suggestion quickly and simply to him: 'Man does not live by Rome alone.'

We smoked. We smoked until our eyes watered and our lips were dry and we ran out of cigarettes, and then he took me in his arms and said, 'I love you.'

15

One evening, when a group of us were sitting together, Shahd Al-Samadi announced to us that she was not ashamed of her romanticism. 'But I repeat that a love of sweets is my chief indulgence,' she declared, her enigmatic smile lighting up her delicate yet strong features.

There was uproar, and then one of the girls took a long drag on her cigarette and said mockingly, 'Down with the cigarette: I am the cigarette.'

They applauded delightedly, then Thurayya said, 'Don't smoke so much or the supervisor will catch you tonight for sure.'

Shahd closed her exercise book and said, 'The new supervisor seems to be quite intelligent and understanding.'

Winking boldly, Samr said, 'She's the same generation as us, so she's not scared of dying.'

The radio was turned on and one of the students stood up to dance amid faint cheers, but the gathering broke up abruptly when someone reported that the old supervisor was approaching our floor.

We put out the lights and took refuge in our beds. We were firm friends, but we made pacts with our neighbours not to overstep the dividing lines between the beds, and not many of us would dare switch the lights on after midnight. 'We've got an agreement,' we would say crossly in the event of such a violation, as we drew the sheets up over our scowling faces.

I felt like having a look at some notes, but was not tempted by the thought of going out to the cold distant study room. Dampness breathed in the air around me, penetrating the thin sheet. Shahd's feet glided over the smooth marble tiles close to my bed and she slipped out with her exercise book. It had to be

Majed Abd Al-Bahi again. At midday when we returned from the restaurant Shahd had thrown her books and lecture notes down on the window sill and shouted that she was a pure bubbling spring which had been confined in a deadly damp, dark well with a lead cover as heavy as a coffin lid. In the middle of the night she would have no prospect of finding anything to console herself with, or of dispelling the nightmare which weighed on her like a lead coffin lid. The two had parted and the affair was over. From now on Shahd would not be late for lectures, forgetful of the time as she chose the right colours to wear, nor would quarrels flare up between her and Thurayya when she borrowed the silk blouse which Thurayya kept for special occasions. From now on his long, supple fingers would not summon her assistance as he explained some difficult point in the class, and passion would not blossom like a magic lantern flooding the world with light and promise for the coming days. An image of Majed Abd Al-Bahi had taken hold of her imagination but in the changed circumstances she had banished it promptly and without hesitation. Betrayal. The form it took, the variations possible, didn't concern her. It was still betrayal, no more and no less.

One day Professor Majed had said to her, 'I'd like us to have a more intimate relationship.'

She had replied with guarded curiosity, 'There's nothing to stop us. I'm friends with everyone.'

'But you're a rare type, different from the other girls. I sense that you treat me as kindly as you would if we were old friends.'

Shahd admitted to me that she shuddered at the sight of the little black hairs growing out from under his shirt sleeve. The prospect of the thick hair on his body underneath his clothes, underneath everything, made her want to vomit. Shahd was afraid of her body and refused to change her clothes in front of the other girls. But fear had been a secondary consideration; her sense of betrayal at his lack of understanding of her was beyond expression. Professor Majed was a recent graduate of Oxford University and this was how the girls referred to him, with interest and admiration. The professor never missed an opportunity to talk about his new plans for the development of the college, plans which he thought himself well suited to put into effect.

Shahd stuck a dried pansy in her album and carefully wrote the name of the flower and the date and the place where it had been growing. She closed the pages and said, 'I'm bewitched by his personality.'

Rashly I asked her, 'What do you know about his personality so far?'

Her words sang a dancing tune as she said, 'He's cultured, modern, intelligent, and perhaps he could love me.'

In Shahd's presence the girls hinted that she was Professor Majed's favourite. 'Don't dare mention marks, because I don't care about them at all,' she stormed.

They sniggered and winked and asked her sarcastically, 'What do you care about then?'

Everything progressed normally, and Shahd grew more confident of her abilities and intelligence, and accepted his invitation to visit him at his home. They cooked the food together, and when he wanted to treat her as a proper guest and make her a cup of coffee Shahd leapt into the kitchen and started to boil the water without giving him the chance to rise from his place. Then she took a book from his shelves and began to talk about it uninhibitedly, showing a detailed knowledge of it: 'You have Scarlett O'Hara too? *Gone With the Wind* . . . Rhett Butler was an intelligent lover but she was a stubborn unyielding girl. She needed two men, not just one. Her beloved Ashley was the embodiment of her dreams of idealism and purity.'

Her uneasiness was tinged with astonishment at his assumption that she was a girl of experience whom nothing would suprise. His mother, wearily moving the white headcloth she wore back off her hair, was in the habit of instructing him each week to marry and settle down. 'Your house is a mess,' she would tell him, striking one palm against the other, then strolling through the empty rooms. 'Your shirts have no buttons. There's dust piling up in the corners. When are you going to get married?'

But Majed Abd Al-Bahi liked liberated, experienced women, and was well acquainted with their special pungent fragrance. Confusion broke out in him when he tried to reason something out which would help him to understand this girl as she really was, and failed. He remembered their discussions in the cafeteria: encounters there were never more than collections of words flying here and there in the middle of the noise and cigarette smoke and the empty teacups scattered about the tables. In the end he concluded that he didn't know her properly, and was losing his equanimity and inner harmony in the face of this enigma, the enigma of girls who behaved openly to everybody, who could be at ease with whatever type of person they met. The girl just kept on talking as if she were sitting in Hyde Park. Sometimes she had seemed reserved and embarrassed when the group broke up and the two of them were left alone, but now she was displaying her talents in front of him, and he was about to find out the special thing which made her different from any other girl. He undid the top buttons of his shirt. 'It's suffocating,' he pretended to grumble.

'Shall I open the window for you?' she asked gently.

'No. There's no need.'

How should he begin with this girl? He got up and pulled her to his chest in a violent embrace. A lot of things happened then, so was it the hardness of her eyes and the way they suddenly stared at him that he would remember most? Or the cry of fright which prompted him to release her from his arms, or her running to the front door, vanishing gradually from sight until all that was left of her was a succession of stifled cries?

Betrayal for the second time. For Professor Majed Abd Al-Bahi refused to speak to Shahd again. He turned his face away whenever he saw her coming, and ignored what she said in class, tossing aside her questions if ever she had the inclination to argue a point with him. Why did he hurt her by this slighting of her when he'd once talked to her of the kindness of old friends?

16

Those automatic clocks in our heads stopped working and we no longer knew what day it was. Was it the sixth day, the fourth, the eighth?

Time flowed down upon us as the blood stains gathered on the concrete floor, whose original colour had been submerged under layers of faded brown and red. Someone brought us tinned food and we ate mouthfuls of it without tasting or being conscious of eating. Where was the God my mother had told me about in my childhood, with a face like a calm, wise old man and a beard which spread across the world in a white cloud? All I could see was a dreadful stony hedgehog rolling brazenly around us, and the crushing blazing disc of the sun shedding circles of light which rained down with the bombs and the bullets, growing wider all the time.

My feet tingled and became numb as I stood constantly at the treatment table. The small empty bottles increased in number daily, and time circled round them singing mockingly: only a little while till you're finished. An old man came in carrying a child who'd been hit by shell fragments the day before. In the dimly lit room, amid the crush of people, the child's hand reached out and knocked the bottle of disinfectant to the floor. A red stream of mercurochrome poured over the floor, tinting it a brilliant red like the red cakes which I'd thought so beautiful when I was a child. There were cries of annoyance and regret and some cursing from round about the room. Without waiting to ask for anything, the old man fled carrying the child. 'He'll come back after a bit. His child's scratches weren't anything to worry about,' said the nurse.

I came to suddenly as if someone was shaking me; the oil lamp in front of me seemed to be swinging violently round and round. A sense of frailty and weakness swept over me, spreading to take in the patch of burnt skin on the back of the man who was lying there without any clothes trying not to moan all the time. There was a smell of dried blood, the choking rancid smell of the toilets, rotten and sour, then the smell of the phosphorus bomb coming from all over the man's body, and the surface of his skin, and his swollen eyelids. Phosphorus is a green dust which spreads like fire through dry straw. I was enveloped by a fit of cold shivering, faces swayed before my eyes and I began to stagger, knowing that I was about to lose my balance. I fell, losing all sensation and awareness. The nurse dragged me outside by the arms. 'The girl doesn't eat anything these days. You'll be better with some fresh air.'

The air outside seemed pure, brimming with oxygen and permeated by the acrid smell of gunpowder. From the door of the first-aid centre I saw Shahd approaching, with her triangular, wheat-coloured face and her hair full of sweat and dust. Her gun was on her shoulder and she wore a red blouse over her battledress. Before I could say a word she spoke quickly and uncertainly: 'I had to wear it to avoid being a target for the snipers on the opposite hill.'

'But red? That would have attracted their attention all the more.'

In the exposed crater I'd been wearing a red dress, and I'd had to cover my back with exercise books so that I was invisible to the aeroplanes and their bullets couldn't hit me.

'This was the only blouse I could get hold of.'

She told me the precious secret which had prompted her to come and see me: 'Shaher. He's in the hills near by. You didn't know, did you?'

I'd heard nothing of him since the battle began.

We used to drink wine at our simple little feasts when Shahd came with me to his house or to the café in the country. She sang traditional songs to us – happy songs and songs of slighted love – in her tender, gentle voice, as if she was a peasant girl waiting for the moon to appear on a harvest night. We expressed surprise at her beautiful voice and, pleased and proud, she said that she'd inherited it from her poor widowed mother. 'But there's no sign of the knight coming to carry me away on his white charger,' she said in mock regret.

Shahd-the-Rain and Lily of the Valley I called her. 'You're wild, Shahd, aren't you? Your relationship with Majed Abd Al-Bahi was a wager you lost: you couldn't tame him and he couldn't tame you.'

With a frown on her face and a bitter smile, she'd retorted, 'Stop psychoanalysing me, Jinan. I swear I'll upset your calculations if you don't stop philosophising.'

This was the Shahd who was afraid of her own body, and yet incapable of indifference in the face of Majed's ignoring her. 'I love life,' she used to say to me, 'and I hate death: the body of a human being swallowed up by a miserable hole in the ground.'

Now, in front of the clinic, she told me sadly about the martyrdom of a fighter called Muhammad Fallaha.

A tank was approaching the Jabal Al-Hussein roundabout. Fallaha positioned the projectile in his RPG and jumped out from behind a wall and moved forward. The tank lumbered towards him groaning and began to open fire with the five hundred millimetre gun. Fallaha kept on advancing without firing. Bullets exploded like metal flies around his face and his slight form without hitting him; in the hail of brass, falling like heavy rain, he continued his progress towards the tank. Twenty metres away he shouted loudly, 'God is great!' and the B7 left his shoulder and hummed through the air. Shahd was watching him as he opened his mouth as wide as it would go, and knew it was something he had to do to avoid being deafened when he released the projectile. Fire blazed through the tank and it became a column of fire with tongues of flame leaping up in a frenzy, consuming the huge metal body. Fallaha said afterwards that Kalashnikov bullets bounced off armoured vehicles like biscuit crumbs, but the B7 went through like a knife. From their hiding place his companions gave voice to their own joy: 'This is your day, Fallaha!' But he shouted back at them, laughing. 'I'm just giving them a dose of their own medicine!' And he bent over the long barrel to reload it as soon as it had cooled down.

Shahd wept and her face grew dark as she recounted how he'd died a martyr's death on the third day of the battle, having destroyed many more tanks before they could sweep through Jabal Al-Hussein.

17

The aircraft was refused permission to land by one airport after another. The world is crowded with fugitives and people who are weary and sad; the only people who would have been happy to welcome Amer's jumbo jet were his comrades, his weary mother and me in my sadness. He had said, 'This civilisation's a whore lying between the thighs of history, who's abandoned us and gone over to them. We should cut her down to size before she destroys us.'

To worship civilization and then reject it is the key thing, according to Amer. An African country supplied them with fuel and food, after refusing them the first time. When they touched down at another airport they were almost out of fuel again. There was no agreement on the hijackers' conditions. To me Amer looked like Tantalus standing in the middle of a pool of pure clear water. Branches of apple trees dipped close to his head bearing their delicious ripe fruit. Amer raised his head and stretched out his hand towards a juicy red apple and the branches lifted, pulling their fruit out of his reach. Amer brought his head down to the water to quench his thirst and the cool gentle wavelets receded and parched earth and dust were left in their place. So Amer remained a prisoner of his eternal hunger and thirst.

If only you would come back, Amer. Come here. Go out and fight and die, but away from this nightmare plane. Give me your famous equations and ask me again, with sarcasm and exasperation, as we argue, 'One and one is how many?' and I'll answer without thinking, 'Two,' and you'll strike my open palm and cry mockingly, 'Not two, clever girl! Einstein's theory of relativity means it could be an infinite number.'

Perplexed, I'll say to you, 'Now you're contradicting yourself. Didn't you tell me a little while ago that one side of the equation is knowing who our friends are and the other side is knowing our enemies?'

But I remember you now when you played marbles with us. You bet on every last one and sometimes you won all the marbles in the street, and other times you were left with none. Then you would aim a big ball of spit on to the steps of our house as you went home empty-handed, shouting that I was a cheat. 'You're stingy. You don't want to risk the ones you've got. Tomorrow I'm going to beat you up to show the others they can't fool around with me.'

I would run away from you clutching my worn cloth bag, resolving to guard the marbles I'd won with all my strength, for how was I to know that you would never carry out your threat?

The road back to my mother was long, and I asked Salima Al-Hajja ten times or more, 'When will will we get there and see her?'

We arrived at the border and the soldiers took our identity cards from Salima Al-Hajja. I remained silent, terrified of being at the border and of the old yellow buildings from where my father had been led away to prison. Jafr Prison was in the desert, and people asking about my father shuddered when they said its name. So she lowered her voice and repeated the details in a faint whisper.

That afternoon I saw her. My mother. She looked different, thin as a thread; she'd never been that way before.

Salima Al-Hajja stared at her with annoyance, concealing her sympathy. 'I suppose you spent every night in tears?' she said to her, and my mother nodded sadly.

The bracelets, where were the bracelets? She used to wear them all the time, and nothing would make her take them off. Gold wedding bracelets with lozenge shapes engraved on them. There had been seven of them and only one was left, but I didn't know how they'd gone until the last one vanished and was changed into cash to buy milk for my little sister.

This time, when we began moving from one house to another with my mother, I grew disgruntled and annoyed. 'It's never easy for people to have guests,' she would say.

There was one house which put us up, where they fed their children apples and peaches behind our backs. When our modest allowance arrived I became the owner of some important property – a bed which in spite of its broken leg was all my own. With great pride I became a pupil at a school near by. I informed the girls straight away that my father was in prison because he had tried to resist an oppressive king; then I told them the story of my mother, and explained to them that the king refused to let the children of the people eat chocolate and imprisoned the fathers who tried to get it for their children.

I thought about the people, us, and about Salwa in exile with her children, and Salima Al-Hajja and our neighbours waiting patiently for feast days so that they could eat sweets. My mother was the queen of the people that I knew.

18

I saw Thurayya in the many-page letters from her which I carried around Beirut in my bag: she sat quietly assembling pieces of ancient pottery from archaeological sites and writing a distinguishing number on each of the pieces to make clear where it belonged when the item was stuck together again. Her job, in the Department of Antiquities in Nablus, was simple and yet exhausting, according to a colleague of hers who had come out on a visitor's permit. He observed that her back had become slightly bent, giving a new profile to her body worn out by constant work. 'We work long hours, too,' he said. 'We don't have the same holidays as them – it's rare for one of us to get a proper holiday.'

On the much-folded, crumpled paper she had written:

It seems that we no longer have any alternative but to write letters to one another or find some trustworthy person who will agree to take a message for us. I hope this doesn't go on for too long. The children often don't go to school and the curfews last many days at a time. If only you knew how frayed my mothers' nerves have become, and how her problems with my father have increased as a result.

Mati, the daughter of the head of the department, goes to great lengths to have arguments with me and to try and provoke me. According to her, we are culturally the lowest of the low, and fit for nothing. Anyway, she's soon to be married to a rich boy from a family of Ashkenazi Jews and so perhaps this will keep her away from me and stop her coming into the department every day.

Believe me, in spite of my close involvement with what's

going on here, I feel alienated from our old friends. Salwa has a new boyfriend every day. Aida's a lost cause and has retreated into her family despite all the claims she used to make, and Samar struts about the town square every day in Cardin dresses and Jourdain shoes.

The colleague I told you about doesn't think of anything beyond himself. As far as he's concerned I'm just something he loves, but in his own special way, a love which is far removed from any relationship that could be translated into reality. He's no longer any more than a friend I turn to in certain situations, but he never fails to do what I ask him, however awkward.

My father's other wife tries to pick a quarrel with my mother from time to time. She puts on her best clothes and sits in the doorway of their house which is opposite my mother's. My mother doesn't talk to me when she's upset, but she gets annoyed with everyone and it's as if she's saying to herself that she earns a living making clothes for people while her husband buys the best of everything for another woman . . .

Hard work and lack of sleep were transformed into a feeling of nausea roaring in my guts. Time stretched out and seemed to doze, sending a dizziness spinning out into the corners of my head, and the stale air reeked of dry blood and the penetrating odour of chloroform, the only disinfectant we had left. Tiredness spread branching along my limbs, my breathing was constricted and I couldn't stay on my feet any longer. The smells and the people crowded together had a tranquillising effect at first but this evaporated as we grew more exhausted. Somebody shouted, 'This is impossible! Where's God? God!'

'Are you asking for God at a time like this? Why don't you ask for your mother while you're about it?' answered the nurse sarcastically. 'Right now you're as far as away from God as you could be.' He let out a loud guffaw. He was like a comedian straight out of a silent film. 'Ask about morale. Our morale is high and that's all that matters for the moment.'

I was helping him dress a young fighter's wound. It was huge and gaping like a toothless mouth. He asked me jokingly, 'Why are you wearing a wedding ring just like mine? I'm old, you're young. I'm running away from my wife and you're chasing after your husband!'

Then he added in a kindly, sympathetic voice, 'But I forgive you. The dressing's finished and that's all you have to do. Go to the door and get some fresh air.'

Fresh air! Oh this fresh air, how hard it was to acquire these days, as unattainable as the Palace of Versailles. When Amer visited the centre he had remarked, 'So you've become a nurse as well? When the war's over Salima Al-Hajja will be sure to make you a white dress and call you "Honourable Doctor". My mother admires all doctors. If she could see you now she'd bring her blue beads and make you wear them for protection, regardless of what either of us said.'

Shahd and I had to leave our positions to go on a mission to a beleaguered area near by. Jabal Al-Nuzha they call it – the Mountain of the Pleasant Excursion – although you would hardly go there for a pleasant excursion: concrete houses are heaped one against another here and there like little matchboxes, and the whirling winds, which are mentioned in the Quran – burning, aggravating, crazed winds – blow over it raising grit and dust.

They had brought in Bedouin soldiers from the heart of the desert who would be unconcerned if the city was destroyed, or so the people in the shelter said. Soldiers with long braided hair, metal bowls for their food and drink, and cartridge belts crisscrossing their chests and fastened around their waists. Weariness flooded through my body as I climbed with Shahd up the rough winding roads between houses hidden in the gloom and open drains where traces of rusty dirty water trickled, and I grew exhausted with alternately running and abruptly throwing myself face down on the ground every time flares cracked the sky over our heads. Because I couldn't see where I was putting my feet I walked into walls which loomed up suddenly in front of us or stumbled into craters piled up with rubbish, stones and old tins. Brave Shahd didn't take fright when a stray bullet brushed the ends of her hair. She drew a solid piece of metal from her pocket, placed it in my sweaty palm and said, 'This is a bit of shrapnel that nearly hit me yesterday so I kept it as a souvenir.'

A souvenir? In times like these, Shahd? Why don't you admit that you're romantic to the core?

The shelling grew heavy so we sheltered in the doorway of an empty house, and Shahd started to whisper.

'What I said to them yesterday turned out to be right.'

'To who?'

'Those people who were sheltering in the cave at the end of the valley. I warned them that if they were hit they shouldn't pour water over anyone burnt by phosphorus bombs.'

She hesitated with studied indifference, and I urged, 'So what happened?'

'A phosphorus bomb landed at the entrance to the cave and a lot of them were burned. They undressed them and covered them with earth until it was safe to take them to the first-aid centre. As a result they were all saved.'

Ah, Shahd, you're a heroine and you haven't just started being one now. You spent years in an orphanage. Your father died a martyr, and the school with its kindly head and its teachers with their hard stares was there waiting to receive the children of martyrs. You wore one dress nearly all the year round, and stood squashed in a queue waiting for your one glass of milk a day. You waited with great patience for a bundle of toys which came once a year from an international charity. You shook out your joy over the brilliant patchwork squares of the bedcover donated by American aid workers and waited, impatiently this time, for the brown paper bag containing a few oranges, a handful of *zaatar* and one cake of Nablus soap, which your mother brought at the end of every month.

The image of the little girl in the clinic came back to me, screaming for her mother with the pain that spread through her when we stitched the wound in her chest without an anaesthetic. It was a fine needle but as long as a knitting needle. I cried out with her and soothed her with the usual meaningless words. Her screams continued. It seemed there was no hope. Our sterile needles had run out, and the packets were scattered about, pieces of plastic filled with air. The world became a field strewn with mines and sharp needles, which grew smaller then vanished. We had to have one needle after another, and quite simply they weren't available. The girl asked for water. Weakly she moved her swollen lips and said, 'I want a drink of water.'

The nurse had given instructions: 'A few drops only. Not more.'

It wasn't long before the girl's eyes closed, and she never

opened them again. The blood in my eyes changed to tears and the tears changed to stones and the stones to huge quarries straddling the hills, incapable of movement. I implored God and His Prophets and the Virgin to let her move but she'd closed her eyes and she never opened them again. I had to cry. I wanted to cry. But the tears solidified like balls of mercury, obliterating the words *What God has willed* from the surface of the golden charm in the shape of a hand, the hand that was found in the houses of all families with children.

She was lying there on a faded, ragged bit of a cloth, a greyish pallor covering her from head to toe, sunk into a state of quiet surprise and extreme tiredness. She wasn't the first person to die in our wretched centre but she looked like somebody who had waited for a long time for life, and then when she had found it, it had flowed out through a hole in her small breast. The breast was like a dark tunnel blocked by a few threads and white bandages which were powerless to stop the warm life-blood seeping from the little heart. Life turned to red, then white, then yellow; her skin turned the colour of the turmeric that old women keep in their cupboards to beautify their banquets. Armies of flies came and settled on this waxen fragment of death steeped in yellowness. A crushing pain descended on my temples and all the faith I'd had in life was dispelled by a bitter sense of bewilderment and disaster. This poor girl was the same age as my little sister. Why couldn't she live?

All the rivers, seas, and oceans in the world were not enough to wash away this stupefying pain, which seemed to taper into thin points with thorns growing on them and puncture my veins like sharp, painful needles: why couldn't she live? Why did she die?

19

Time was flying apart, white birds fluttering over the open sea then landing shrieking on his little aircraft which had broken down. As the minutes passed his cigarettes and food and water ran out. The Little Prince had gone to fetch help, but couldn't find his way back to him. With a violent gesture of disgust Amer pulled the flying helmet off his head and his face appeared from behind it. Waves of tiredness passed over his eyes, spilling out into the words he spoke: 'I'll try to attack it. I'll try to wipe it out even if it is a city asleep. Sleeping cities and ancient newspapers.'

He lifted an ancient newspaper from the wrecked cabin and read, 'The sea is in front of you and the way out behind you.'

It was strange to be having a dream with my eyes open. A drizzle of white vapour was falling around my eyelashes, and my head swirled with thousands of ropes of light, long threads and longer ropes intertwining with one another. I returned to my dream: I found you dead on the road to the sea, and your mother Salima was there beside you wearing the long black dress of the women of Jericho and wailing and shouting. I was frightened of her dishevelled, streaming hair and I ran away from her, back to my mother and father.

To try and shake off these visions which hurled themselves at me like a raging sandstorm was futile. According to Shaher they were a result of my unsettled childhood and came when I was depressed, but which of us hasn't been unsettled in his or her childhood? What about you stealing an orange in the camp at Irbid and getting the stick on the palms of your hands until the blood ran, or Amer crying and crying for a pair of leather shoes to go through the snowdrifts in, during the winter of the first exodus? The tears froze in the corners of his eyes and at the ends of his fingers and toes, but his crying did nothing to stop the painful frostbite in his extremities. We are our past, and it can catch up with us whether it runs after us in plastic sandals or leather shoes; it makes no difference.

My head was an orange, ripened by the sun's rays on one side and mildewed and rotten on the other. I wanted to wake up. 'Look,' Shaher used to say, 'reality isn't frightening. The only really terrifying thing is running away. It's true that things are no longer as clear as they were at the start, and some of us are happy to doze away our lives in romantic notions of the revolution rather than living in the reality of it. The age of Sultan Abd Al-Hamid is over, and the present age will mean the end of us if we don't learn how to be part of it.'

Hesitantly and with some confusion I put to him the question which preoccupied me incessantly and leapt into my mind without warning: 'When will we be involved in the real revolution and not just be on the sidelines?'

'There are a lot of questions to be answered, and none of them is straightforward, but the existing situation doesn't offer us any quick answers. There's one indicator which gives me some reassurance and that's our work in the camps: the children here grow up quickly without asking many questions. The one certainty is Palestine. That's the word which is real, first and last, and it's there in a glass of water, in the boys' shorn heads, on the doors of the houses and the old wooden windows, at the fingertips of the girls who marry young following tradition, in the barrels of the guns which the Young Lions carry when they're on guard at night and in the toothless gaps in the mouths of the old people.'

It was the tenth day of the battle. 'Shaher's not here,' they said when we arrived in Jabal Al-Nuzha. 'He went out on a mission. He'll probably be back soon.'

Shahd and I had gone there to prepare first-aid equipment; at this news happiness suddenly seemed a ridiculous notion which had vanished deep into the world's unfathomable interior. Families crowded together in the corners of the shelter and the wailing of children rose up on all sides. Some mothers, unable to control their irritation, slapped their children but still didn't manage to silence them. The constant prayer in the dry mouths, moistened only by a few drops of the scant water which remained, was for bread. The men present begged us to share their food with them. Tinned meat without bread. 'Fine,' said Shahd, but I made do with a bit of yellow cheese.

Perhaps I'll never eat meat again after this, I thought.

Human flesh flying about, blood and dead bodies made me feel sick. What a failure I was as a nurse. Reality itself had become a nightmare of flesh, living and dead, warm and cold.

When I was summoned to the headquarters in the evening, I found Shaher with them. When it came to it, it was difficult to believe that I was really seeing him. We smiled at one another both at the same time, all we could do separated from one another as we were and surrounded by the misery of war, and the world which was sinking day by day into a hell of shelling and gunfire rose like a bow pulled back taut and firm from the bowstring.

'I was on my way to try and see you today,' I told him, 'and I was caught in some crazy sniper's fire. I flung myself down on the ground and the bullets from his machine gun blazed over my head. When he stopped shooting I jumped into the first doorway I could find and a bomb landed on the very spot where I'd been standing. I couldn't go out that way again so I dug my way through a back wall of the house and got out the other side.'

'Listen, Jinan,' he interrupted, 'this position is surrounded and we're in a critical situation here. We may try to withdraw to the eastern side of the city even though our chances of getting through the blockade are very slim.'

The darkness surrounded us from every angle, and the oil lamp was about to go out. Now I had him in front of me and he was going to leave again straight away. They were all absorbed in making the necessary arrangements. I didn't weep aloud but the tears poured down my cheeks without stopping. There wasn't much hope that the withdrawal to the eastern hills where our men were would be successful: they weren't given more than a twenty per cent chance of getting through safely. I began to feel a burning in my nose and eyes, and my face became a damp, dark, painful mass. I groped my way in the gloom, more impenetrable than ever now that the oil lamp had finally gone out, and touched a piece of coarse material which turned out to be the apron belonging to the mistress of the house we were in. I rubbed a bit of the wetness off my face. My eyes were closed, and my ears took in the sounds which flew among the rooms and passageways. The whirlpool of faint noise sucked me closer to its quickening revolutions and I dropped into it like an old blind spider who'd lost its way.

'There won't be any more death from now on, will there?' I asked him. 'You can understand wars, but not death. Death is too hard to bear. Things won't get any worse, will they? I'm not staying here. I'll cross to the other side with you.'

He touched my face and said very calmly, 'You're not coming with us when there's nothing for you to do and, besides, it's too risky.'

I was silently aware of some obscure disaster approaching, far away at first, then moving close.

'What if something happens to you?'

'You'll rearrange things in a new pattern and plan your life to make sure that you go on growing and changing.'

'But I'll kill myself if anything happens to you. I won't live one second after I know you're dead.'

His voice came to me sounding weary, but full of affection and gentleness: 'You'll take care of yourself; the world doesn't end with the death of one person. It's a vast place and somehow it affords us the space to hatch desires and then work to realise them.'

A voice was calling, so he promised to send a note to Jabal Al-Nuzha to tell me where he was; then he went away and all I knew was that I would wait until we met again, regardless of the destruction and upheaval that went on round about me.

The sails and the clouds were motionless and the sea was a blue expanse stretching away as far as the eye could see. Amer relaxed on the comfortable aircraft seat and pulled the attaché case up on to his lap to make room between his legs. The music they played in aeroplanes was slow, commercial too, seducing the passengers to wait patiently and lulling them into a state of calm. What sort of calm was it? Cold and deadly or hot and energetic? He could hear his heartbeat pounding noisily and fiercely in the base of his skull where his head rested on the foam cushion. He raised his head and looked behind him, checking the position of his two comrades. Everything was normal. The world is normal and we alone are abnormal in their eyes. In a little while the aircraft will be transformed into a ball running from the dry land down into the sea if they don't release the prisoners. Everything is ready and calculated in advance. There's no scope for haggling or retreating. Here I am realising the dream of my exodus; for the first time there is a clear justification for it and it glows more brightly. Since our childhood they told us to flee and we fled. We fled day and night, from Beersheba to Hebron, Hebron to the Balata camp in Nablus, Balata to the bridge. Amman. Paris. Cairo. Baghdad. Damascus. Kuwait. Other places whose names were sometimes familiar and sometimes not. In order to stop asking questions we had to begin providing answers.

Amer looked at the clouds advancing round the aeroplane, snow cities built in the air. The smooth white expanse makes you feel like walking on it. We walked on clouds for a long time and now we're regaining the confidence we lost in their wars in order to begin our war, on our terms. This is our own war and this aircraft's only an early stage of it where we're securing our comrades' release from the enemy's prisons. Calm, calm, that's all we need. Calm which is cold and deadly and hot and bitter and concentrated. Calmness and patience. Didn't they tell us to be patient? Have we not been patient for so long that patience is the one skill we have which is worth exporting to them? We have all forms of patience and calm: September, May, July and all the months of the year, and all the days of the lost years, and we will hand out the important dates of our history to them.

The moment of departure. White lights glowed in the cockpit through the round porthole of the aircraft. A white light. White. Then the departure. A light drizzle of rain drew perpendicular lines on the round window. The aircraft tilted, then straightened out. 'From here I make a right angle with the world,' said Amer, and announced into the microphone that he had taken control of the aircraft, asking the passengers to remain calm. Calmness came before everything else; his two companions would be responsible for the rest of the arrangements regarding the passengers. 'I promise you that I won't harm you, but I and my comrades are acting on behalf of our country and for the release of our prisoners.'

Firmly and with confidence, Amer turned and asked the crew to change course.

Joy imbued with the delighted numbness of victory. Only five minutes ago, they agreed to hand over the prisoners . . .

The chessboard stones were transformed into coloured pipes through which warm water percolated. The cities had given in to the conditions of Amer and his comrades, and Beirut was like an oval pool whose waters were olive green, dark green. I want the mint green of the fields of Jericho and the water falling in shining drops on the banana leaves and in long splinters on the dark asphalt. The hateful chessboard houses are black and white. There are big flats and little ones. Music dances in the stores and humanity groans under the weight of their bank accounts. A fly dances on my shoulder, the only creature capable of dancing, and the words run under the keys from right to left, from east to west.

When this work's done, I'll leave all these papers here and forget about them. No, I'll do it now. I picked up my bag and went down. The lift was quicker than my sluggish thoughts. What was going to happen now? What could happen, I wondered, after the past and before the future? What's definite is that you're in the fast lift of a new building in a city festering with cafés, restaurants, businesses and tourist attractions. I laughed to myself. Tourism, that was the problem. In Amman houses made of solid stone from the hills had been demolished and then restored; how would they be able to restore the great masses of glass in the high concrete walls of these buildings, and could the tourist industry risk them coming down on their heads?

I amused myself by looking in the shop windows, and it seemed to me that they provided a screen to shelter the city's rich inhabitants. This one was winter: furs, coats, hats, and stoves made of cardboard with the 'wet' clothes displayed around them to 'dry', and chestnuts scattered on the floor; and this one was summer: silk, muslin, and flowers uprooted from nature and arranged in their plastic, paper or glass versions. In this city nature began and ended with the shop windows. As I went along, I passed by the window with the red dress in it and shuddered slightly. This red was a gleam of joy and desire, but it also awoke a fear buried deep inside me. Ah . . . Hebron. Salima Al-Hajja's house. Once I heard them talking of the men who'd been hanged: all were clad in red, their strangled bodies bleeding from within, their tongues like pieces of red meat dangling from their mouths. They talked of the smell: God, that smell, as the excrement slid from the men's pants in their terror and the sudden shock of fear. I imagined going alone into the sitting room with its red curtains; one of the hanged men would be dangling there, to poke fun at me with his sticking-out tongue. Then he would go with me to my death, asking, 'Why are you afraid of me? The king's horsemen hanged me, so why are you afraid of me?'

I glimpsed my reflection gliding slowly along close by me in the shop windows, and I remembered Shaher who had passed this way and scoffed: 'They bury themselves in trite books and pretentious clothes and money and perfume, and polish and smooth their bodies twelve hours a day so that they gleam brightly for the other twelve hours. This street is the shop window, a vast display for two worlds that never meet: one spends hundreds of thousands on putting illuminations in the streets for the nights of the feast, and the other curses the feast because the snow and cold come with it.'

There was a smell of dust-laden damp and a light rain began to fall, the drizzle of summer's end. I took shelter in a passing service taxi and became aware of a gentle, hoarse, regular sound: tick tock, tick tock: the windscreen wipers were two hearts beating gently without pain. Tick tock, tick tock. The pain seared me like caustic soda on bare flesh: Amer swung on the end of a thick rope and Shahd was encircled by drops of light sparkling on the lily of the valley which surrounded her on all sides and threatened to smother her; and I in this chaotic jumble of noise and crowds was listening to two hearts beating.

Sometimes I was afraid that I would look in front of me and a huge monster would rise up out of the desert earth carrying a whip, and start to chase me.

Exile. Nothing is as painful as exile; it stretches ahead into the future, and back into the past, and bursts through on every side at the places we've dammed up with the dry straw of memories.

In that month in mid-summer my father insisted on staying. If it was a choice between Jericho and a quiet life, he would choose

Jericho, of course. The planes circled above the camps and the orchards and the tiled roofs. He went to the police station to ask for arms and came back with an ancient rifle with the date 1917 engraved on it. But a friend of his came on foot from Ramallah and said to him, 'You're free to decide that you want to stay. But what about the girls? They're a big responsibility.'

'In that case we'll leave,' said my father to his friend, who was covered in red dust and dirt from his journey. 'Yes, we'll leave.'

They called to me to hurry down to the car. 'We'll be back in a couple of days. Don't worry.'

I wonder if they believed what they were saying. I tried to think of something to take with me. Only a short trip, then we'd be home again. When they called me a second time all I'd picked up was some nightclothes, a fountain pen and a photograph of my mother. In the car, as it rumbled its way along surrounded by groups of people hurrying on foot towards the bridge, I realised that this was going to be a longer excursion than they had envisaged. I reached out my hands to uproot my yearning as if it were a troublesome weed, and refused to let myself look back: I had left Paradise behind me and taken hold of the gates of Hell and I mustn't look back again.

In Amman in the middle of a jostling crowd in Salt Street, swept along by a never-ending flood of sweaty, submissive, dust-stained humanity, I noticed people gathering at an alarming speed before a small speck on the ground. The crush grew denser, cries of ridicule and disgust rose in the air, and in the thick of the swearing and the punching a police car horn sounded several times. There was a foreign girl there shouting and crying, but nobody was listening to her. A mini skirt. Surely you know what a mini skirt is! It's everything and nothing. 'It's the reason why we're defeated over and over again,' said one of the passers-by.

The police freed the foreigner's bare legs from the mêlée of outstretched hands open to grab them, while she went on mumbling words which met with no response.

20

The new land became the target of constant air attacks. In Amman, Irbid and Salt they started to come without warning. Vietnam became the day-to-day focal point of our inspiration, in the acts of heroism we heard about, in the books we read, and in the rooms and corridors where we argued and studied. It was said that from its yesterday Vietnam created its tomorrow, and we with this today of ours were carving out the future. We exchanged news and books and papers about Vietnam with enthusiastic fervour.

Shaher had written his first letter on a little piece of torn paper:

> It's the early hours of the morning and I'm in a border village whose name I haven't heard before. It's a peaceful village full of barrels. You might not believe this but I keep finding barrels – or what look like barrels – all over the place. Barrels for water, oil, washing clothes, bathing, collecting cattle dung, everything, perhaps for making love in too. I'm sitting in a Land Rover and writing in a drowsy light, and the wind is blowing wildly like a demented jinn. And you . . . sleeping or telling Thurayya thousands of stories? But the one picture that I have most strongly now is that you're dancing, dancing wildly, your body trembling. Have you broken your chain, Scheherazade, and begun to accept the world which scares you with its peaks of pain and fulfilment and tenderness? I'm full up with you and with pagan desires. Do you forgive me, O gentle goddess moving around in the clouds, frightened of slipping towards the quivering jelly-like earth? Do it. Tread boldly on the earth, and forget everything that brings back

the resentment you felt towards the old worn-out idols, because it's we who are smashing them. There's nothing here but the first battalions of rain so perhaps I'll go out among them and let them wash me thoroughly.

21

He would come towards me from the head of the alley. The soil began to change there and become darker in colour, denser and more solid, losing its fineness among the numerous deep craters.

He would come. His face would be the lamp to light up my childhood and I would remember the pink organza dress my mother used to put me in for feast days and weddings, and he would come . . . I would snatch the commas and full stops and question marks from his face and put them in my pocket, out of my wits with love.

One day I would dare to do it: to run down the long street dancing, twirling round in circles, and fling away my briefcase whose sedate serious look I hated. I would sing unrestrainedly, let out whoops of joy like Native Americans when they won great victories, and then I wouldn't feel the burden of depression and the fear of dismal isolation. Loneliness wouldn't press on my chest with its crimson fingers interlacing, making me dizzy, almost suffocating me.

He would come and perhaps I would walk along the street barefoot or naked, it wouldn't matter which, without feeling the need to hide my inadequacy and weakness and sense of deprivation from this huge city. I would pluck the skyscrapers from the ground one by one and stand them on my fingertips, and perhaps I'd get hold of some acid to dissolve the cold ugly concrete surfaces. But if I woke up in the morning and I was alone, I would find him there like that obscure bird, the griffon, who in the legends only appears for the reckless adventurer Sinbad. Sinbad may have been foolhardy and impetuous but he knew how to keep his ship on course through the whirling lashing waves. How can I demolish the explosions of passion, the flying splinters of strident love, when I'm a woman from Jericho who has been wandering distractedly around unfamiliar streets since the first captivity in the days of Joshua, son of Nun? In the beginning the questions brought us together but soon they were the very things which separated us:

'Jinan, you can't accept the new reality around you. You haven't thought of building new friendships which are firmly established inside you. All right, we know all about your roots, but all you seem to do is remember the world you used to inhabit, and you don't bother to construct a substitute for it with the idea of prolonging its existence.'

'You, dear friend, have a spirit of heroism about you which I can't touch. The past, Shahd, Thurayya, Amer, Salima Al-Hajja, the concrete walls of our old house in Jericho pull me back all the time. I can't trample on their images and construct new ones.'

'You . . .'

'You . . .'

But the reality was that our concerns were no longer the same. He had gone beyond the past and I was still embedded in it. He searched on the radio for news bulletins and commentaries, while I considered these a repetition in a new form of all that had gone before, and tried to find music and singing. He believed in the possibility of shaping a new life while I felt the pressure remoulding me more slowly and making me more prone to waves of doubt and readier to discriminate against things and people around me. So I found myself pulling together all these feelings which were making me distraught and trying to reconstruct them by working with people in the camp. Only among them could I breathe peacefully, and then the private misgivings which were paralysing me and disrupting my thoughts evaporated.

I jumped over the open drain where the water moved sluggishly, giving off a smell of rotting fish bones and newly tanned leather mixed with the slime of coagulated rubbish. In Umm Ahmad's house I found her eight children eating bread soaked in gravy out of a big roasting tin; they reached out and gathered up the morsels in their fingers with eager haste, all except for the youngest, Samir, who lay on the cold concrete floor on his bare stomach, his legs scarred with bruises and grazes. I picked him up and brought him to her, and said anxiously to her, 'Umm Ahmad, if he likes feeding himself over there why don't you dress him in something that'll cover his bare stomach?'

Umm Ahmad looked twenty years older than she really was, but her astonished laughter transformed her face.

'Let him get used to it, Jinan. People get used to everything in time. How can you be so afraid for him? I pity you when you have naughty children of your own!'

And we began to bicker, her confident bellows of laughter and my uneasy little giggles puncturing our dispute. 'But that won't do, Umm Ahmad. Of course everything's possible, but that's going too far.'

We arrived at a compromise solution where neither of us was the winner or the loser. She went along with my suggestions for a limited period until things went back to being as they had been of their own accord. Then once again the baby's bottle became a football at the children's feet or a dart flying through the air. The hen strayed down from the roof, tiring of her coop, and wandered among the mattresses on the floor leaving her droppings as she went. On the rare occasions when the coffee pot was washed with soap, it was usually as an extra gesture of welcome and hospitality for my benefit.

Life went on and I visited every house and ate olives, onions dipped in salt, and bread. But I was powerless to solve most of the problems which dogged their lives and made their faces cloud over with worry.

Of course I had no thought of being a social reformer, but our work continued to suffer from a lack of cadres. No sooner did the girls we had working with us begin to feel confident than their families rushed to marry them off, fearing that their interests would be harmed by gossip. The particular circumstances of the female comrades called for more careful thought and study. Those who'd escaped either a romantic or an arranged marriage inevitably suffered from their fathers' pigheaded attitudes or the narrow-mindedness of their relatives. Those who stayed on regardless had to become experts at first aid, civil defence, political propaganda, publicity, social education, and at the same time remain on good terms with everybody. This meant doing constant exhausting work and always being prepared to put up with considerable losses and disappointments. So Subhiyya, who'd been detailed to work in Farahaat, which was a relatively large area, was going to marry a joiner and go with him to Saudi Arabia. Muna, who'd returned from a nursing course in the Soviet Union, refused to work in the clinic and went to one of the big hospitals as a receptionist; she wore a gold bracelet of interlocking square links and a gold chain from which hung a little ivory horn set in gold, a gold key and a tiny diamond heart, sent to her by her cousins in Africa. Fatoum, the seamstress, hadn't yet married though the skin on her face had gone dry and coarse because she put so much pale face-powder on it; as a result her bad moods became more frequent, she quarrelled daily with the other girls and almost failed the dressmaking course we'd taken so much trouble to arrange for her.

I felt an inexplicable alarm when I met Umm Dawoud one day and she began waving her arms about and shouting because her son had lost an arm during explosives training. My colleagues were so taken up with small details that the important issues became confused or were overlooked altogether.

Sometimes, among the watermelons and mounds of potatoes for sale, people became wrapped up in a wedding ceremony or a funeral and forgot a politics study group that we'd pinned our hopes on, so that in the end only a handful attended it.

The questions came thick and fast and the answers were slow to arrive and inconclusive. All I could do was absorb more and more details, so that I would know when our eyes were properly opened and how we could keep them as bright and wide open as possible.

22

Time stretched monstrously ahead of me; it formed a circle, enclosing me for all eternity. Today was the twenty-fourth of October and Thurayya would be thirty. I used to joke affectionately with her: 'You're older than us. Five years older means many years wiser. "A day older and a year wiser"; so the proverb says, Thurayya.'

Thurayya would moisten her dry lips with the tip of her tongue then say, 'But it's my family's fault. They sent me to school late. You're mean, Jinan, because you always do me out of enjoying my role as the older one and make yourself responsible for me. That means that you must really be older than me.'

God, how much more aware than us she was of the passing of time, how she counted the days and months like any stupid child. She took her sandwiches and ate them outside the restaurant strolling about under the pines and cypresses. She wore white knee socks and did her hair in two pigtails tied at the ends with white ribbons like a little schoolgirl.

His name was Jaafar and he wasn't a regular customer at the student cafeteria. Thurayya fell in love with him and found herself turning into a cactus with spikes and thorns to keep him away, as if she didn't want him. 'Why are we so scared of men?' she asked me bitterly. 'Is it a legacy we inherited from our mothers and took in with their milk before we were conscious enough to ask questions?'

Inside I knew she was also thinking about her father who had sold sweets on the street and turned himself into a matchmaker, leading his daughters one after the other into marriages of which they knew nothing in advance. I asked her, 'Why are you always so full of misgivings? Why do you begrudge yourself a bit of happiness and pleasure?'

The lights from the corridor outside shone through the glass in the door of our room and she answered me in a troubled whisper, 'Do you know, I hate all the lousy philosophy classes that Professor Sophocles gives us.' (Sophocles was the name we used for our skinny midget of a teacher when he annoyed us with his endless babble about action, power and false logic.) 'But what I really like is that philosopher who talks about boundary conditions. Boundaries. Heavens! It means that they're conditions so clear and sharp and penetrating that they give their name to all that's gone before and all that's to follow. I honestly don't like the melodramatic situations which arise in connection with Jaafar, but I'm hopelessly in love with him, and I can't handle it. I'd grown used to the problems of my father and his wives, but I've always found it strange to accept another person into my life with that kind of affection which dissolves all traces of defensive behaviour. I feel cowardly and hesitant and scared to death that I'll expose myself too much. What shall I do if he doesn't love me back, or if he pretends to love me and then implies that I'm chasing him? You love boldly, Jinan, without asking questions, and that's what I can't do. I have this constant picture of my family and their problems, and it always stops me seeing my own situation clearly. When I think of my mother weeping and wailing and having nervous breakdowns I just can't think straight. They'd take me away from college and lock me up at home if they knew I loved him. A boy without a degree or a respectable job! Heavens above! My father's stupid fat wife would ridicule me, and my mother would go crazy because I hadn't got a rich, respectable husband like her rival's daughter. I feel as if there are worms boring into my head making me think a whole jumble of things, and some of them make sense and others don't.'

I left her to face her private torment, but it was enough for me to observe her when she went to the cafeteria. She bought two bowls of crème caramel and invited me to eat one of them. She put the other to one side untouched and I asked her if I could have it. Faintly but firmly she said, 'Finish yours and go away. Keep your hands off mine.'

I opened my mouth theatrically and said, 'Look. I've got a

worm in my upper molar who needs another bowl of pudding to fill him up.'

She wrinkled her forehead between her thick eyebrows and said, 'I'll spit in my bowl if you don't go away. I told you to leave me alone now.'

'Ah,' I remarked in tones of mock reverence, 'the flying Jaafar is about to arrive and I should withdraw. I hope you know some good long stories to tell him so that he'll stay.'

At this she swivelled round in her chair to face the buffet wall, but she turned her head from time to time to stare fixedly at the entrance like a frightened cat waiting for the local bullies to attack.

It was always obvious to me when these meetings were going to take place: if Thurayya made her normally unkempt hair look softer and more feminine and tied it with a pink ribbon, if she hid her glasses at the bottom of her bag at the end of the lecture, it meant that she was expecting him to roar back into her world. According to what she told us, her heart pounded dreadfully and she felt every drop of blood as it pulsed through her until he arrived, a tall young man with tousled hair around his face in a halo of black curls and strands which somehow looked longer than it really was, his first smile suggesting at once that here was affection without an object looking for the warmth it knew was hidden in a corner somewhere.

Thurayya came in one day holding out her hand to show off an old-fashioned ring with a turquoise stone. It slipped about on her thin brown finger and we laughed at how loose it was, until Shahd hurried to get a long piece of thread which she bound around the back of the ring to make it the right size. Samar, who wasn't as close to her as the rest of us, commented sarcastically, 'I wonder what museum the gallant knight could have got it from? Did you really believe him when he told you that it was a keepsake he had from his grandmother?'

A look of anger and irritation appeared in Thurayya's eyes but Shahd hastily interrupted the taunts, clapping her hands in joy and laughing with mischievous enthusiasm, 'Long live romanticism! You're the romantic now. I renounce my title completely.'

Thurayya had made her first step. Where Jaafar was

concerned that refreshing impetuosity of hers became stronger and more spontaneous.

Sometimes as we drop into the blackness of night, sleep coming to us slowly, calmly, deliciously, we are startled by the sound of something falling, and our feet are drawn to it, numb and unsteady after being tired for so long and then relaxing. Then, all at once, as if the bottom step of the staircase is missing, we are plunged downwards with a violence which jolts us back into wakefulness. I gasped disbelievingly when Thurayya told me, and she responded with a strange severity: 'No one but us needs to know.'

Wanting to make certain, I asked her, 'So he's not like us and the rest who belong to student organisations? If he carries a B7 and goes across the river on suicide operations it means that he's above the arguments and the little everyday missions.'

The black circles grew deeper around her eyes as if there was something eating into her and consuming her with a terrible fire. I wonder how time stretching away into the future can be as confining as a steel suit of armour, rust-proof and impenetrable. The calamity made its appearance in a report brought to us by one of our friends. Our room turned into a wailing wall down whose little steps rolled our griefs and heartbreaks and Thurayya's shrieking; she was afflicted with bouts of hysteria which made her tear up all her papers and books in the midst of her weeping and moaning. Her cry of despair was huge, like the stray bullet which had pierced his skull. After the nurse had gone away and the injection of sedatives had taken effect we realised that something anonymous and grave, against which we were defenceless, would always pursue us, something bigger than the explanations and more profound than the awakening of a pain which didn't go away. Perhaps Thurayya had believed that he was alive up till this time, for they'd stopped her seeing his body – the only way she could possibly have grasped his sudden death. He had been buried in the martyrs' cemetery as the Israelis wouldn't allow his family to accompany his body to Sebastiyya. His sudden death separated him from the white columns of Sebastiyya with their smooth sides tinged dark red by the influx of thousands of mosses slipping in across the current of time as it rushed blindly on, always in the same direction; columns of a uniform roundness under a sky which moved between them in blue rectangles and ovals.

After a week the nurse stopped visiting Thurayya and the pain burrowed deep inside her. Our unspoken anguish and silent grief disfigured us. Gone were the evenings of discussion and noisy, joking laughter. Our horizontal classifications which had stretched like a straight line dividing the world in two, the part we liked and the part we hated, went round in circles. Grief and sorrow and bitterness interfered in our lives. The guest in the cafeteria was gone, and confronted each day by Thurayya's constant crying and the sight of her permanently knitted eyebrows, which grew wilder-looking around their tapering ends, we began to feel as if our room was encased in a girdle of stone.

One morning Thurayya got up and made us the slightly sweetened coffee which we loved. This was a good sign. She'd stopped doing anything like that for ages now. She looked in the mirror for the first time and announced to us as she braided her hair, 'I hate gunpowder and bullets and fragments of metal which kill human beings and I shall never again take part in any struggle which uses violence as a means to achieve its objectives.'

'Even our revolutionary violence, Thurayya?'

'Yes, even our revolutionary violence, girls.'

23

From the window of the house the vendor's tray, stacked with fried pastry balls, came floating into sight along the road; a small cluster of flies hovered constantly around it. The wife of Hashem Al-Taraash sat at the door of her mother-in-law's house and her clean damp washing hung on the clothes line which stretched the length of the wall. Always there was that same smell, something strange and obscure mingling with the smell of earth sodden with the soapy water emptied out over it by the women. The houses merged into one another and spread out like slanting rays of light. The way the dwellings were grouped in Shatila indicated the different areas which the inhabitants had come from. In one direction an alleyway led to the houses of the people of Farada, in another the various dwellings of the people from villages in Galilee like Majd Al-Kuroum, Al-Mazra'a, Tarshiha and Sha'b were visible. On the headstones in the nearby cemetery they wrote, 'Here lies So-and-So from Haifa'; 'Here lies So-and-So, daughter of Such-and-Such from Birwa'; they brought their identities with them, deposited them on the cold marble, and slept.

The voice of Umm Mahmoud scolding her daughters trickled into my room: 'You stupid girls, you try and make yourselves believe you're really living in Beirut. I know you put your address as Beirut when you write letters. The address deceives people in any case. If I was as empty-headed as you, I could carry a handbag the same as the *mukhtar*'s wife and strut around like you do in tight trousers. Don't think I don't know what goes on inside your heads, you lazy creatures. You kid yourselves you're city girls. I wouldn't be surprised if you refused to work the land if we went back home – there's always one of you sitting here eating all day long and not lifting a finger to help me. Anyway, there's plenty of time, and I'll keep after you, even though I know you think I'm simple and don't understand anything compared to the people in this city whose shop windows you never tire of gazing into.'

I heard a creaking in the yard of her house and waited for the familiar banging of the wooden door as she came to take refuge with me as usual and complain about how tired she was of her house and her daughters and their demands. But all was silent next door and I pictured her there crying silently, then busying herself with housework and not letting anyone see her face until the tears had dried. When she finally came I would say to her as I always did, disregarding the sympathy I felt for her inside, 'It's all right, Umm Mahmoud, calm down. The girls have a hard life, and you put up with more than is humanly possible.'

At this a couple of tears would well up which she would try hard to conceal, brushing them away with her calloused fingertips. Regaining control of her emotions, she would answer wearily, 'Where can I get money for the things they want? How can I plan their lives properly? With a piece of land you give and take. But you spend money here and get nothing back. Abu Mahmoud earns two hundred pounds and I'm damned if I know how we can live. Where are the vines, the olive trees, the apple harvest? O mother, we had such prestige and our children only know sorrow! You study and understand these things – we old ones remember Palestine and remind our children of it, for who's going to guarantee to us that they won't forget it if we don't return in our lifetime? I swear, this generation is rotten to the core.'

'Your daughters aren't as bad as you think, Umm Mahmoud. Things are changing and time's moving on.'

In an apologetic tone as if she was trying to express more clearly why she was upset, she would continue, 'Daughter, before these fedayeen existed we were forbidden to knock a nail into the wall. Five years ago Salem Al-Taraash's daughter threw some water out over her doorstep and the police fined her twenty-five pounds for breaking the law. My house was flooded when it rained heavily one winter and Abu Mahmoud kept quiet; he couldn't as much as knock a nail in on the roof to patch up the wooden boards without a permit from them. Daughter,

I'm the first to rush off on a demonstration singing at the coming of the fedayeen.'

O Umm Mahmoud, you always take refuge with me just as I take refuge in your abundant motherliness when I'm shattered by exile and loneliness. But it's impossible to convince you that the afternoon is the one time in the day that you can relax; you come to the adult literacy classes in the Women's Centre with a bowl of rice to pick over or *maloukhiyya* leaves to shred for soup. I wish you'd come and see me now. When will I hear the ring of your voice and feel my pain and misgivings being pulled away from me, just as a wave rolling up the beach is divested of its scum and seaweed?

24

Amer dominated the radio now. I knew everything about him and paid avid attention to the details about his activities which they broadcast between the intermittent news bulletins. 'What's daring isn't merely to hijack an aircraft, my dear, but to make the passengers and crew sing and blow out candles to celebrate the birthday of one of our comrades.'

There was nothing odd about you convincing an airport tower and hostile troops to send food to the aircraft to feed those on board; what's sad and cruel is that you got this cake with candles and decorations. My dearest wish now is that you and your comrades survive and that you don't have to die so that the operation can be brought to an end before the first round of killings begins. I wonder how you sustain your calm manner during your constant addresses to the tower and your calls for the plane to be refuelled. The first time they complied with your request and gave you just enough fuel to make a one-way trip to the next place. That was why . . . No, I don't want to imagine, or to anticipate, or to think or be sad. The single, inglorious option I possess now is to wait. Waiting is a big square from which we might emerge into a circle of hope. It's enough for me at the moment to be on the shared boundary between the two. We who are waiting can do nothing but wait. Come here, absent one, and answer me. Your stubbornness and pride are all the answer you can give. Is our pride alone a sufficient response to the long years of hunger and humiliation? You will challenge me now of course and say, 'Pride is life.'

O yes, pride is life and more. To survive and to preserve your existence, however firmly the square you have chosen is sealed. 'Sealed more firmly than my eyes or your eyes can perceive,' you say. 'We're on opposite sides of an equation; your eyes aren't my eyes, but we're both bound by the final circle.'

But the final circle sits spreadeagled over the two opposing sides. Your existence is my existence in the largest sense, so why are you trying to die like this? Our principles are the same, and there are many different routes to take, so why should this square be more firmly sealed than your eyes or my eyes can perceive? Why don't you answer me?

25

The dismissal notice that arrived one morning had the condensed wording of a telegram. Shahd gathered up her belongings and left without trying to enquire why she was being sacked. She knew all too well anyway, and the men from the intelligence services had been trying for some time now to push her into a final and decisive fall. With irritation and scorn she remembered the pot belly of the important official who'd proposed to her, showing off his numerous cars and luxurious house to her as incentives. 'I will never accept him, however much my mother begs me to. They want to destroy my world by having me dismissed from every job I manage to get. Fine, let them if they can. If the world disintegrates I'll pick up the bits, and perhaps I'll reconstruct it just to annoy them.'

The heads of the intelligence officers rolled before her, as they fell one by one. She pictured her uncle with his coarse face and the big mole on his nose, badgering her and trying to catch her out, then insinuating that he would throw her and her mother out in the street – his was a decent home and he was the respected owner of the Amana greengrocery business – if she persisted in being so stubborn and refused to confess and turn over a new leaf. 'There's nothing to it, girl. You go to them and tell them all you know, then they give you a bit of paper testifying to your good conduct. You can't do better. It'll take you to a top job in a posh school. Surely you're not content with teaching in these wretched state schools, and being humiliated and followed around by them all the time in such a degrading way? Or you could lie to them and just tell them a bit of what you know, and still come out of it with your head held high and a good conduct slip in your hand. To tell you the truth, if you carry on without one, and in this ignominious situation, you won't get a job anywhere.'

Shahd passed her hands in front of her face in a nervous unsteady gesture; she was afraid to go back to the house in this state because it belonged to the uncle she detested, with his harsh, inaccessible air. His daughters were simple and naive, happy whenever guests arrived because it meant they could have another cup of coffee with cardamom, and her own mother never lifted her prayer mat from the clean cold tiles except to spread it out again and unload on to it the cares and sorrows accumulated over a long stretch of time. She would count the beads of her rosary in the dawn light and, weeping, ask God to let her repent and be pardoned. She would submerge her daughter in her pitiful attempts at showing affection and tenderness, then fire her eternal maxim at her: 'Educating a girl brings nothing but trouble!'

If it weren't for the things Shahd had studied at college, according to her mother, she wouldn't have acquired a head which could split a rock.

Shahd wrote:

Your letter reached me on the first rainy day this autumn has chosen to send us in Amman; autumn is already moving far outside the city in the direction of the fields which we dreamt of walking through together again. Once upon a time you told me that distance and time change a lot of things and make them dry and cold and, I would say, inappropriate subjects for discussion as well. In circumstances like these, which have seen us driven out of our country and hounded wherever we go, times which must be worse than any we'll see again, I wonder how we're meant to talk about anything, little or big, when we can't even mention things in letters because we're afraid they'll censor them: everyday life, I mean. And yet all we have is these beautiful close friendships of ours, and they're the only thing whose beauty I'm more profoundly aware of now. The summer holidays this year are going to be dull and bleak because I'm alone here, you're abroad and Thurayya's in the occupied territories. Oh, these separations! They're ridiculous and so sad!

Often I find myself in really stupid situations and it's as if

I'm incapable of understanding what's going on around me. If you feel humiliated inside yourself it makes everything hard to deal with, and of course you know what it's like when you can't find a job. But things flow smoothly again when I go to Baq'a, to help them in their efforts to build a people's clinic. My encounters with some people there created awkward questions for me, which I didn't know how to resolve. I began by co-operating with them and when an opportunity arose for them to participate and contribute, they were happy to rely on me. I don't know how things got complicated later on. Then, gradually, I learnt not to be so stupid, and to make clear exactly what I wanted from them, without flattery, and without having to depend on general good feelings. That's what helped me in the end to value the contribution of those who see our plans as part of their hopes and dreams, and think that the restrictions imposed on me by my gaolers here are an unqualified testimony to my strength of personality, my pride and my ability to get around.

Oh, Jinan . . . I am constant in my feeling that those who are like us will be able to confront evil as boldly as they confront the best things in life, and that from the ugliness we will be able to create another kind of beauty whose principles will be established in the heart of the everyday and the ordinary, and the things imposed on us against our will. Perhaps our sense of pride is part of the great love which draws us towards our country.

At the end of the letter Shahd had drawn a laughing face and written the word 'Smile' above it in English. I remembered a friend of my father's who was interned in the middle fifties because he'd sent a letter to a friend beginning with a line of poetry: 'If the people want life one day . . . fate will have to respond.'

So don't worry, my friend; at least we're in a better position than they were. Our dreams will always be like pink candy floss that you're free to eat how and where you like, but that dissolves rapidly in your mouth, leaving behind a sweet, heavy taste.

26

The road began to abandon its straight lines and right angles where it intersected the long lane. The lane started at a lofty quinine tree and ended among a cluster of alleyways. Along both sides was the heaped up rubble of the Tabba' joinery works and car repair garages, and a little way off on the right rose piles of refuse – bones, rotting vegetables, scraps of material, old papers – adorned with the black clumps of flies which had gathered in swarms since the beginning of the week. I breathed in the stench of rottenness, the smell of decomposing matter, burnt metal and sawdust.

Suddenly a memory came to me of Samar emptying a bottle of famous French perfume over her hair. I tried to picture how she would look now, the wife of a well-known engineer living in Detroit, giver of excellent dinner parties, member of the charitable organisations which collect donations for the third world. In a brief letter she'd informed me, 'It's not true that racial discrimination exists here. My black neighbour has a better house and car than I do.'

We all shared the same room at college, and sometimes she was nicer than we'd thought possible. The barriers we'd put up when confronted by the daughter of a feudal family tottered and fell in the face of her sustained efforts to approach us, but she used to ridicule us when she was angry for one reason or another; in the spells when we were all happy together we would say to her in a burst of thoughtless exuberance, 'You are our beauty queen!' and warm tears would sparkle on her radiant face, her laughter would come in gentle waves, as if rocked by a mysterious happiness, then she would say with great enthusiasm, 'You're all beautiful too. There's nothing more beautiful than your glowing colour, Thurayya, and your eyes, Shahd, are amorous and alluring like the night. Jinan, your smile says to the moon, "Let me take your place. I know more of joy and sorrow than you, poor thing." '

We used to overlook a lot of things about her and just remember that she was our friend. Once we proposed to crown her hair beauty queen as well. Dazzled by the compliment but scornful too, she said, 'Hair! Are you serious?' and we answered with little shrieks and gales of laughter that we were, and that it would be fun to do it just once.

One year she invited us to a memorable birthday party at an elegant restaurant whose wooden walls gleamed yellow in the light of red candles. At the head of the table sat Samar's friend, Salim Al-Shakery, in an expensive suit of a small dark check cloth. In high spirits we talked and joked and the atmosphere became friendly and intimate until Salim started to harangue us one by one: 'You don't take enough care of your appearance, Thurayya. You're always wearing those jeans. They're so much a part of you that if you were lost in a crowd they'd lead us straight to you.'

Then he directed his arrows at me with a strange mixture of sympathy and coldness: 'As for you, you stupid little thing, you won't stop looking at the world in your frivolous way as if it was a doll that you could bend in your fingers with the utmost indifference. I don't know what would make you more sensible and serious, especially now that Adel's gone away and you didn't manage to establish a good relationship with him.'

He was about to address Shahd who was staring at him flabbergasted, as we all were, but Samar gave him a hard look out of her honey-coloured, kohl-rimmed eyes and for her sake we hesitated to show our annoyance openly.

Then we took out our presents. Shahd had brought a string of shiny bright-coloured beads which she presented to Samar laughing and saying, 'They're like the necklaces I loved as a child, and used to dream of wearing when I saw women in their wedding outfits in the village we came from.'

I gave her a book and said, 'These are Neruda's poems to remind you of the times we used to pursue you to try and get you to read them with us. Anyway the book's written for hunted people everywhere, and so it's dedicated to my nagging you as well.'

Then Thurayya held out a record, mumbling that it was Samar's favourite music. Salim Al-Shakery had no alternative but to join in gradually, in some confusion. 'But none of you have seen my present yet,' he said.

He tore the patterned wrapping paper off a small cardboard box and took out a mirror in a frame inlaid with ebony and ivory. On our way home we saw a young boy climbing a tree, and at the top of the tree the polished face of the moon in a frame of ebony and ivory. Samar looked at it and her happiness was complete.

27

A wave of hot wind got up, lifting with it the dust-laden dampness of the earth. My feet sank into the sand which was a light coffee colour turning to dark brown in places. The lane began to thin out into a sloping line; the walls of the buildings crammed together on either side were varying shades of pale, their colours faded in the sun and wind and rain. The smell from the open drains floated upwards; their contents trickled along on either side of the lane then came together in a single small channel dug along the middle. From the central channel water pipes branched off, straight, slender dark grey cylinders. A sluggish liquid flowed from the doorways of the houses, brown changing to black or green, and formed small scattered pools in some of the shell holes.

At the beginning of our alleyway the air was fragrant with the gentle, kindly perfume of Umm Mahmoud's jasmine bush. It always provoked an unexpected reaction in me, a sudden fleeting restlessness. There would be a fluttering between my ribs which threatened to erupt, but then abated as soon as I had gone a couple of steps along the alleyway. Perhaps it was Jericho rising up in my memory in a spasm of nostalgia, like a gush of steam from a kettle. But Jericho was more than a handful of jasmine or a vast expanse of green citrus groves. It was a symbol of a time of lost love, and a charge of fire and mud and water through the limpid canals where we used to dangle our bare feet.

With each day that passed the scent of the jasmine became less pervasive as the girls picked the flowers and threaded them into necklaces which Umm Mahmoud's youngest son carried wrapped in moistened sheets of old yellow paper to sell at intersections and near pedestrian crossings.

28

The road began to abandon its straight lines and right-angles, and I found your love again in the fragrance of the snows crowning the mountain tops where you had gone, even though I couldn't reach you there. I felt like a prisoner still . . . against my will a prisoner of little details and of an explosive burning pain. I felt as if there was in me this peasant woman with her little pieces of gold-and-silver-worked embroidery which she dared not look at for fear that her emigrant lover would forget her in a distant land and never return.

You were the one who went a step beyond me and brought the fire in you under control, and turned it into ice to build your fortresses and carefully planned defences, and that's why I began questioning you non-stop about where we were and when we would reach our goal.

'There are still some deep-rooted anarchistic tendencies left in you,' you said to me. 'Do you expect all our aspirations to be realised in one fell swoop? Why do your desires and emotions make you feel so frustrated? I don't want to seem to smooth things over, but isn't it enough for us that we're not stuck in one spot, that we're moving forward in all different directions?'

You shook me violently, admonishing me: 'This is a difficult world. You'll have to learn to put up with it. Your romantic ideas will stand in the way of your understanding the reality we're living in, if what you want is a revolution which will swallow up mountains and bury buildings by magic.'

With an effort I went on down the alley. The children were outside playing with broken dolls, and Pepsi Cola bottle tops and old orange peel that they'd picked out of the main drain.

I listened to a number of news bulletins which didn't mention the hijack operation. Hell! What was going on in the silence? The news agencies, the aircraft itself and the hurrying feet of the people who prepared the forthcoming news reports, were all silent. It was the silence of indifference, and God, what a dangerous silence that was. I relied on glances, expressions, as I crawled among the shell holes, straining to see around me and continuing to wait. I ran over to the window and looked out. Nothing. Everyone was continuing to wait as usual. The neighbours were waiting for the approach of evening so that they could call their children in to the low houses. Hashem Al-Taraash's wife crouched in a corner of the passageway giving the brass pump of the paraffin stove a number of hefty strokes to make it burn more fiercely, and the old watchman had let his head droop on to his right shoulder and was snatching a short nap as he sat at the office door.

In the drowsy silence of the setting sun a torrent of memories rushed in on me. For some reason I felt compelled to take out my old records from where I'd stored them years before. The rain may betray us, memories too, but music never. I put a record on the record player which I'd managed to mend after the soldiers had broken it in September 1970 in Amman, but which I hadn't had the heart to use since those days. I'd embalmed it and the music imprinted on those black circles in a remote corner, and left them untouched.

'Everything's all right, isn't it?' Shahd used to say, staring at me with concern and a lack of comprehension, as I played the same piece of music over and over again.

That September alone had reduced music to military marches whirling around in my head, and had robbed it of its association with dreams and relaxation and ecstasy. Now the world was shrinking into itself again and broadcasting songs of blood and pain and dull dejection. I felt I had to retrieve a pure world where happiness was complete as in childhood, and a fleeting smile or the ghost of a breeze in the air from an unsteady memory of Jericho could make me rejoice: Jericho, left behind on an empty car seat while the planes took possession of the skies which dissolved in comets and meteors of burning smoke and napalm.

The light sparkled through the lacework of the curtain and

was reflected on the wall. Hundreds and thousands of little intertwining geometrical shapes blended with one another and formed a beautiful picture of the rays of the setting sun. I sighed. Much as I hated the sunset I couldn't help loving the last flickerings of light from the lamp of the world which broke into pieces every evening.

Little details! He would ask me, 'Why do the little details bother you so much? It's as if you're dealing with the world for the first time.'

For the first time. That's right. That's how it always seems. I'd been protected from having dealings with the world by love, by traditions, by wishes and hopes, and had seen none of the frustrations which were to come.

'It's not a crime to feel anxious,' he told me. 'We all do. Nobody's sitting there smiling when there are Israeli planes overhead every morning. But we're doing something. Doesn't that give you confidence? Why do you stand by yourself in the middle of the road having this one-woman tug of war? You're going to pay an awful price for preserving unspoilt dreams if it makes you so edgy about everything.'

I'm only tempted to be edgy, as you put it, when I'm alone, never when I'm in the Women's Centre with Umm Mahmoud and our other neighbours around me, and I'm teaching them to dress a wound or read and write. For centuries they've been denied the chance to read and write, so that they can't write letters to their nearest and dearest, according to their families. I'm fine when I'm looking at the map with them, picking out the names of the towns we've lost, or when I'm absorbed in explaining the political situation, and all the time they're cursing leaders and kings and rulers all over the world.

When we were small we used to hop over big squares, trying to land a stone in the middle of a square, but we only get to know the game of truths when we're grown up. Why do I try to withdraw to the squares of childhood? At school they taught us that zero was an empty quantity which meant nothing, and that our native land was a collection of beautiful elegies in our composition books which we shut away out of sight when we closed the books and handed them in to the teacher. Since then we'd found out that in the new maths zero was a constant which didn't go in the negative column.

I heard the whispering of Umm Mahmoud's long dress as she approached and pushed open the door. She cleared her throat and came towards me with her gaunt, brown, severe face and her copper-coloured hair twisted into short curls on her temples and hanging in a thin plait under her white headcover: 'Good evening, daughter. Come in and see us for a bit.'

'In a little while, Hajja. I've got to tidy up some things here.'

She went off, letting out a peal of satisfied laughter like cymbals chasing the setting sun on its way. She enjoyed chatting, blinking her short eyelashes or chewing on her stern lower lip, as she regretted something from the past that she knew now she'd never have back. She spoke about her fine quality pomegranate trees as if they were about to sprout up there and then in front of her, then broke off all at once without any intake of breath. She would play with the children who lived in our alleyway and spoil them, then shout at them for no apparent reason; after one such episode she admitted that they'd lit a fire with some straw and wooden boards and this had reminded her of the smell of dried roasted wheat – *farika* – of harvests gone by. Proudly she bragged to me, 'Do you think revolution was discovered in your day? Our revolution was fierce and passionate and it lasted many, many years. It if hadn't been for the shortage of arms they would never have defeated us. Your generation knows nothing of life, my daughter. What have you experienced apart from minor problems and scuffles and little wars? Have you ever seen the sea at Jaffa? I used to go there with my neighbours on moonlit nights and not a soul dared come near us when we swam fully dressed and spent long nights on the beach with tambourines and a lute and drum. Our citrus groves spread over the earth's palm, places of infinite treasure where children climbed the trees and ate green almonds and apricots and played with the sheep and hens and cockerels. Don't you want to hear about the oaks, the medlars and the red plum trees?

'Our weddings were truly joyful celebrations and not artificial, bad-tempered, bitter occasions like they are now. Would you believe that they almost set fire to my veil on my wedding day because they lit so many festive candles around the arbour I sat in? I suppose you think the cinema's a great invention but you missed out on a lot of other things that were nicer and more interesting than the cinema. But my crazy daughters believe I'm a feeble-minded old woman who doesn't understand anything about the city and new things. At the moment Hiyaam keeps asking me to buy her some trousers that are in fashion – Charlton or Charleston or something. She said all the girls at her school wear them, so I said to her, "You be careful. Get down to studying your lessons or help Jinan and her comrades with the work they do. You'd be much better off." '

She'd gone and I remained standing near the window, resting my arms on a shelf on the wall. A scrap of shrivelled sheepskin lay on the floor under my feet. The sound of water knocking in the broken tap connected me to the kitchen – a fertile source of cockroaches in the night – and the far corners of the room piled high with books, some of which we'd read and some not. Time is treacherous and deceptive. I'd said to him, 'I'd like to read them all, but time . . .'

All our small scattered things were pervaded by his unaffected laughter blossoming and reaching out to my face and my waist and my fingertips: 'Time . . . time . . . so why doesn't the sunflower wait a bit longer instead of being so dreadfully impatient and tense?'

I tried not to be angry at his affectionate banter, and I tried not to complicate any more issues. But silence is also treacherous and deceiving, and the aeroplanes might come at any moment and destroy what we'd built. Of course that wasn't the whole world, but it was this portion of it which belonged to us now. He would have called me a coward if I'd said what I was thinking, so I always kept quiet. It doesn't matter that we're afraid, but it's important not to let this fear get the better of us. I knew and he knew so why make things more complicated? He won't be coming today, I thought, he won't be coming in his military jacket and brown cap with dry mud clinging to the heels of his shoes asking insistently for a quick cup of tea. 'Strong, very sweet tea. Not the English way.'

'Why are you away from me so much?' I would ask him.

'Why don't you ask Moshe Dayan about his troop movements? That would be more efficient than asking me, anyway.'

'Oh Jesus, why don't you stop making fun of my emotions?'

He answered me then, but he didn't really talk, so why couldn't I stop clinging to bunches of miserable words like a hungry man clutching a loaf of bread? His attention wandered away from me to an old newspaper, then he burst out laughing noisily: 'Did one of the letters you're so good at waiting for actually reach you? I'll make you change your job when we go to our own state and you'll have to stop being so attached to words and letters from the past. We'll set up new things there. Perhaps we'll find a new husband for that daughter of Umm Mahmoud who sulks at her mother's all year round because her husband's lazy. Perhaps we'll convert the big houses there into youth activity centres where they'll learn to enjoy the pleasures of life which we've been denied for so long.'

He went on flicking rapidly through our papers and letters, then called me excitedly, with tender sarcasm: 'Quick! Leave the tea and come here!' – for I'd abandoned him for five minutes – 'Look, this is one of the letters I wrote to you when we first knew one another. My beloved, lost among the typewriters and envelopes, didn't I assuage your thirst for letters that day?'

He held the sheet of paper out of my reach and would only give it to me in exchange for a cup of tea. I read:

> I get a sense of a destroyed childhood when I see her and my eyes cling to her with her short hair and her laughing eyes. When she laughs I know that she's suffering more than ever, and because of this I can only picture her in pain like labour pains. She gives birth to new life with her constant questions. I hate to think of her as a pure, naive person; I like her up to her neck in mud, carrying the burden of experience and of her passionate enthusiasm in her delicate fingers. This is why I feel more and more strongly that her childhood was spoilt, and that her suffering is the deepest and sweetest kind of suffering.
>
> I don't know if I've begun to love you, but I love myself and the world when I'm by your side. I listen to you and consider you to be the most truthful of women in a world where the women are more deceptive than your laughter – and is there anything more deceptive? Don't fall in love with me, don't treat me as your wonderful child. Nothing fills me with confidence, but you hating me. I find I don't like anything at all except listening to you and you listening to me. I always said when the new Rome was burning, 'The sea is dead.' For

the first time I see the sea truly being born; for the first time the sea isn't dying.

After a final snort of laughter he became calm and earnest again and said to me, 'When two people are getting to know one another in this world, what do they need apart from a few silly words so that they can communicate and get rid of some of the shit we're all rolling about in? Why do people want eye contact to come first, then tortuous introductions, before the two corpses finally get together, done up in cellophane like boxes of chocolates? Shiny wrappings are vital to them because they're dripping with embarrassment, and they hesitate a thousand times, declining at first, then accepting after they've tied themselves up in the complexes of the East and the endless haggling between its men and women.'

I remembered one of the men saying to me with false sincerity, 'Please don't be angry, but I'm curious to know why you're wearing a scarf over your hair?'

'It's quite simple,' I'd answered. 'My hair's dirty and I haven't had time to wash it. The other female comrades are doing more important jobs than me and they wear scarves over their heads all the time.'

Then I wondered to myself what he was getting at. Was he offering me his views on matters of hygiene and honour and chastity? 'I'm sorry that my scarf reminds you of the era of female seclusion,' I went on, although I would like to have replied, 'You ultra-progressive man, would you prefer us to wear either khaki uniforms or eastern dress so that you could easily distinguish between us and categorise us and give us pluses and minuses?'

I thought bitterly, 'Is it a coincidence that this same man sits in the office with his feet up on the window sill while one of the girls washes the floor, and pays her not the slightest attention and doesn't even think of fetching her some clean water?'

The shoe seller doesn't lie. Al-Taraash doesn't lie. Umm Mahmoud doesn't lie either. The grocer lies occasionally. But the liberated souls in the thick of the revolution say very little that's true sometimes.

I moved the needle on the radio dial this way and that, scared that I'd miss a news report without being aware of it. I heard Amer's laughter mocking me: 'You're so superior when all's said and done. Why don't you accept things for what they are? Why are you waiting for me to extricate myself when I'm in the process of achieving my freedom?'

'The freedom to make mistakes is nothing but a wasted effort in the end, Amer.'

I imagined him smiling his hard, heavy smile in my face: 'But the freedom to cross unimpeded into your native land comes before anything else. Do you want us to arrive there with our comrades still in the enemy's prisons? Do you think we can walk over the bodies of thousands of martyrs without falling like they did?'

'But isn't this operation suicide . . .?'

He turned his face away from me angrily: 'That's just your opinion.'

Amer, the tribes have separated us from our childhood. The divisions and subdivisions are still coming down to us from earliest pre-Islamic times. Their names and languages are lost in the desert and on the high seas. You raise two fingers in a victory sign through the porthole of the aircraft, but who are you signalling to? Which way are you directing it? Which wind are you trying to catch?'

29

Time poured down in a libation to thwarted desires. The desires of stones, of water, of love, of impossible answers yearning for questions. Amer was doing battle with questions coming towards him in armoured cars, soldiers with their heads swamped by metal bowls, and signalling equipment transmitting messages between rooms firmly anchored to the ground and others flying above it.

What were the questions then? The clouds, those snow cities fixed in mid-air, had moved higher up and further away since the aircraft engines had unexpectedly broken down like this and its hijacker - who was a former professional engineer, as the radio broadcasts commented - even with the help of the three crew members on board was unable to correct the fault. And then the co-operation between the other aircraft and the troops on the ground had reached a peak now.

Amer drew the safety catch from the bomb and trembled, a decision taking shape in his mind. Now the trick had been exposed, now hopes that there could be a deal had evaporated. For would the gaolers offer the choicest meals their prisons could supply for the sake of ordinary people whose fate didn't concern them and whose deaths would just constitute extra fences for their iron prisons? And they were going to repair the aircraft, were they! What tricks were they up to now?

Dozens of faces revolved in front of him in a spiralling circle moved by a single thread: when would the zero hour be? They huddled in their seats, bathed in sweat and hot dust, and their hunger began to return with the anxiety and the waiting. Momentarily it seemed to Amer that something united him with them, for tension threatened to creep up on him as he wondered when he should begin the countdown to zero.

If I went to Umm Mahmoud's house I would become immersed in the little details of their life: the big bed on the right, the rug with its traditional Arab pattern spread out in the middle of the room; the single cushion which Umm Mahmoud would insist on taking down from on top of the mattresses in the alcove so that I could sit on it; the oldest of her daughters coming in with the big tea tray loaded with little glasses with faded engraving on them; Abu Mahmoud silencing us with a dignified gesture when an important news item came on the radio. But could I face it tonight? I would wait here by myself, I decided, for while I had the feeling that I was growing less anguished this was mixed up with an enormous sense of confusion. I lay down on the bed. On the brink of sleep I paused and woke up again because I suddenly had the sensation of my foot slipping towards low spongy ground where it would be impossible to keep my balance.

Calm smiling faces of children from Sabiha in Jericho revolved around me; they were aiming a ball made of some flimsy material towards a little goal they'd constructed from rough stones. There was a long-drawn-out cry of agony as if the pain of a chronic illness had lived on in my memory, and then I seemed to know it was the little girl screaming before she died. Thurayya's bewildered face took the place of the little girl's face, then the tracks of the Israeli tanks rolled into view as they circled the town square in Nablus. I thought of Amer and how he and I had fought as children over a reed pipe which Salima Al-Hajja had made. I stopped myself shouting out loud, 'Where is he now?'

The spiralling circle plunged down from the top of one of the chessboard and stone buildings, and at the entrance I found his shattered body in pieces and the blood streaming around his eyes and his neck and down his legs. Nausea rose in my throat and my stomach, and when I tried to raise my eyelids all I could see was the same dark bloody liquid. I knew that I had to wake up properly. One or two candles were still alight, lingering on from the oppressive clinging world of my dream. I got up and hurried over to the light switch. Its blaze dazzled me, etching small circles which hovered like flies around its glow. Does love prevent us from seeing the tragic wounded faces in the world? The banana plantations were intensely green, the broad leaves of the plants dipping towards the brown earth and meeting the pure blue of the sky around them. Ruby clusters of dates, small yellow-red balls, dangled from the long palm leaves to the pages of the newspapers with their huge red headlines.

Tomorrow they would write about him, and I would remember a peasant woman carrying her son who didn't want to go back home. The woman was Salima Al-Hajja. I recognised her as she picked him up, winding her strong arms around his legs in the patched trousers which had belonged to his father and which she had taken in so that they would fit him. Waves of the flowers they called 'madflowers' billowed in wild disarray over the doors of the houses in Jericho; sometimes they called them 'beauties'. On the plains around the camps of Jericho the wheat flourished, its stems erect and strong, separating the camps from the Moab mountains and the Dead Sea. Then shacks made of concrete and heaps of gravel and stone grew up in the alien towns. 'I can't see anything which is my native land,' I said to him, and I shouted to the empty air.

'The more agitated you get, the faster you move your hands while you're talking,' he remarked.

I looked at him without sorrow and said, 'This isn't the Jericho that I left behind.'

The sound of car doors drowned out the military marches as the cars' owners loaded up their belongings and drove away. They drove away to the past, and the mirage formed at the side of the road, inflated by the scorching heat of the hot sun. Their ears were pricked, waiting to hear the splatter of the napalm which was pouring down on the heads of the people on the valley slopes.

I shouted out loud; the pain took me by surprise and the tree trunks squirmed but it made no difference to the bird stuck to the birdlime. We always quarrelled about the same thing: I said to Amer, 'Put the birdlime on the holm oak,' and he ignored my suggestion and put it on the terebinth tree. When we'd made up our quarrel we spent the day nibbling medlars and waiting for the twittering of birds to come from the thick branches daubed with birdlime.

They said to me, two days and we'll be back. I felt angry and sick thinking that this story about going back, which we'd heard on all the broadcasts, had been our downfall a thousand times. Two days and we'll be back. And I only had time to look for my fountain pen and a photograph of my dead mother. There were people dotted about in the sea at Jaffa exhausted and reeling with the joy of arrival. We walked over the railway line which lay parallel to the Mediterranean coastline, and some of us arrived somewhere and others didn't. The road went off at a right angle, and I stood exactly on the corner and began trying to reach both sides of the equation. The equation and its two opposing sides, that's the heart of the matter, Amer says.

I moved about restlessly in bed. The radio had been silent up to the moment my foot came into contact with the rolled-up pillow. I tried to wake up properly. 'The whole planet's got the smallpox,' I said to him. 'The WHO reports are wrong. I've known it for ages.'

Reality. Reality. You say it all the time. See if this reality can relieve the pain that's suffocating me now.

The knocking on the wooden door became increasingly violent. I opened my eyelids with difficulty; they felt like the sandbags we'd filled the day before to make barricades. I jumped up hastily to open the door, muttering bewilderedly to myself for the thousandth time. Umm Mahmoud stood before me and the moist dawn revealed clearly the uncertainty written on her forehead; she said, 'They're asking for you, Jinan. Go to the office: Shaher's been wounded and he's in the hospital.'

30

'Where? How?'

'There was a roadblock. A roadblock we knew nothing about.'

'Did the fairies put it there?'

'No, that's not what I meant. We know who put it there. But we didn't find them when we went to reconnoitre. They want to get us out of the South and they think incidents like this will have an effect on us. The official confrontation hasn't begun yet. But the main thing is that Shaher managed to keep driving the vehicle till he reached our post.'

In spite of the hail of bullets, Shaher had kept going through the unfamiliar roadblock, so unexpected that there was a chance it was the only one. They said, 'It's as well he went on, because he would have had it if he'd hung around.'

I gazed at his weary sleeping face, not wanting to wake him. The nurse said, 'He's still in some danger. He'll regain consciousness in a little while.'

In a little while. The little while was an age, all of time. I saw his features and it was like the first time, or as if I hadn't seen them since way back before a succession of mornings and evenings, and days following one another like the ancient codes of Hammurabbi. His tousled hair lay matted on the pillow. It had grown longer than usual and was dark, when before it had been chestnut. Instead of being pale, his face had a slight blue tinge which made his skin look browner. His broad hostile mouth was closed and looked small, like the mouth of a little child whom sleep has taken unawares.

I waited. The black burning squares loomed large before my eyes, flashing incessantly. The circle revolved in the main square in Nablus where Israeli patrols, orderly and quick, marched round and round. When the demonstration began people gathered, and small boys came carrying piles of tins and stones. Thurayya, who had sworn never to take part in any violent activities wherever they were, was distributing Palestinian flags which her mother the seamstress had made out of red, green, black and white material. Thurayya, daughter of the aged seller of sweets, with her hesitant uncertain ways, was rushing along in the wake of dozens of other human beings, suddenly assailed by feelings of anger and rebelliousness and a desire to protest. She'd been able to come out of the smothering darkness and the desolate sense of loss and begin to do something. Are these fearful beginnings hard, I wonder, when you know the endings will be bitter and destructive? Gradually she'd been aroused from the limbo she was in and realised that the death of a martyr hadn't cancelled out her existence. 'Experiences accumulate, Jinan, they accumulate, and shape us without us realising it.'

This message came in a letter delivered by her student friend, whom she'd seen off, staunchly and unreproachfully, to Beirut. Students like him came from the West Bank in droves each year to the universities in Beirut and when the exams were over they returned with new commitments and different interests.

'And I for my part,' wrote Thurayya, 'am beginning to practise restraint. A minor attachment can begin with a brief laugh, then turn into constant hell later on. Our relationship hasn't got a name yet. It's partly unrealised love and partly just ordinary friendship. But the main thing is that our true selves won't have been given as hostages in exchange for the real thing which didn't happen when it was supposed to. Do you think we can go on being captives of this eternal game of love when it sometimes seems such an insignificant part of being alive?'

As I waited, I was engulfed by a feeling of joy which had been no more than a hidden gleam hovering uncertainly inside me: he was still alive. The air strikes, the bodies staggering under the impact of the shelling, the shrapnel embedded in human flesh, the searing burning phosphorus bombs, the violent tremblings of earth and air which shook people from head to foot and made them deaf, the cries for help pouring from behind locked doors and windows in September in Amman and the black weapons behind the annihilation hidden in the dark – all this had passed him by and he was still alive.

'Death wasn't an abstraction at the Battle of Karama. The flesh of the dead was torn from their bones when I came out of the meeting room, and I saw three of our young men lying in their own blood. I recognised a close friend of mine: he was lying in the square and his lower half was a charred mass, but his upper half was completely unharmed and his bright eyes looked out, full of astonishment. Can you imagine how strange it is to encounter the astonishment on a man's face at his own unexpected end?'

'This destruction all around makes me different, changes who I am every day,' said Shahd, forgetting to extinguish the glowing cigarette end in her fingers until its heat slowly scorched the skin around her nails. 'I can see the walls of our old world tottering and the heavy boots of the intelligence men trampling on our wounds.'

The triangle of her wheat-coloured face framed by its coal black hair appeared before me now, as she said earnestly, 'Do you realise, Jinan, they're stealing the joy of a lifetime from us, as well as our everyday happiness, with the iron chains they keep hidden in their pockets?'

Events had wrapped me around in a dark cloak of fear and given me a sense that the world was without pity. A cold shudder ran down my back and reached out all over my body. A hospital waiting room. Old magazines and leather chairs veiled in wrinkles which crisscrossed them in all directions. A glass door, an ashtray and a wooden table standing firm on its four legs. Everything seems to have a solid presence except the fires of our sufferings and our grinding sorrows, endured in silence. I pushed away a feeling of terror which I knew was beginning to show itself in my white face and my cold hands whose nails were tinged blue. White, blue, grey. I was standing alone against time which was stuck fast and showed no signs of jumping forward to take him and me beyond the danger period.

Luminous dreams of the past flooded into my head. The leaves of the palm trees growing by the wall of our house in Jericho move in the breeze, and their sharp edges graze me. Clumps of reeds and bamboo plants dip their heads on the banks of the canals which cut through the plantations. Barefoot, I hurry over the big cold tiles in the Greek Orthodox Church square; Amer is about to grab the hem of my dress and I run faster, afraid that he'll win our game of blind man's buff. In the distance a vision of the sea appears: brown, mauve, green, blue, turquoise; and the sun's rays dance on its surface which is tinged the colour of molten lead at evening time. I ask with a naivety Salima Al-Hajja is unable to reply to: 'How can this sea die just because ancient history and school text books called it the Dead Sea?'

'A sea or a lake, it makes no difference,' says Amer.

The main thing is that it shone and sparkled before our eyes when we stood up on the roof of the house to see it. A single lemon grows on the tree against the wall and I breathe in the perfume of the white blossoms which cover the trees in the orchards as far as the eye can see. My mother, preoccupied with her tasks, calls me through the open window, 'Don't pick it, girl. Leave it to get bigger. Don't do what Umm Masoud's daughter did last spring.'

Was it still uncertain if he would live or die? The question clogged my throat and I dared not ask it openly. I wondered about all the medical equipment. It was the only tenderness in the afternoon, a soothing balm against the shellfire, the gunpowder and the burning. Nurses came in and out of the room. The question hung uncertainly in my mouth, and one of them signalled to me to be quiet, then whispered, 'We'll know his condition in a little while.'

Umm Mahmoud came to stand behind me, wordless and grave-faced, without the headcover she usually wore in the presence of men. She stood there awesome and calm, waiting for a harvest from a faraway piece of land and cursing the exile which yielded nothing but humiliation. Her dignified silent stance made me think of weddings in the past when she'd danced round in the bridal circle clapping and singing the traditional songs, wearing a kerchief embroidered with pearls:

Who's this bridegroom parading along
He of the pampered life of ease?
Congratulations, Mother!
It's a peasant girl he's brought, if you please.

I hear her repeating in a bitter, anguished voice, 'Our white days have turned black, and we've forgotten the songs. The blackness has covered the white.'

She put a gnarled hand on my shoulder, full of cracks like the trunk of an ancient olive tree, announcing with this gesture that she would wait with me. She was there behind me, and in front of me the squares joined and formed a solid mass, then spread out into separate units: the cave where we'd hidden, the King's horsemen, the police station at Jericho and the blue stars of David fluttering above it, and the napalm scattering death and destruction. I remembered a schoolfriend of mine who died during the exodus. She was my playmate in the streets and squares around home as well. We used to call her after a famous film star and she would close her book and laugh, her joy overflowing in cascades of delicate splendour. Death was a black coffin, but napalm was a sudden shock of burning which ended in charred ashes and nothingness.

From out of the biggest square the Hebronite appeared, Salima Al-Hajja, who had nourished my childhood with her beautiful legends. The ghoul had vanished with the coming of the electric light, the jinn lurked in dark, forgotten caves, and Salima Al-Hajja spent her old age on the doorsteps of government departments in Amman, demanding the release of her son and the other Black September internees.

The squares knitted together, and I walked out of them into the middle of the angle, its sides became parallel, met again and finally became perpendicular. From there I jumped out into the hospital waiting room.

'Not yet. It's not time yet,' the nurse told me. His breathing was slow and irregular. The sound of his quiet voice thudded in my ears as I remembered a day we'd walked by the edge of the sea. 'There's no access through the Arab towns. The only way open is via us and the sea.'

Us and the sea. The horizon coils up at the end of the sky, then the aeroplanes come and the radio stations bring us military marches and news of an unprecedented defeat. When we began it was September and there was a thirst which they'd tried to create as night was created to follow day. In September the big chairs moved backwards and forwards in an uneven circle. An upheaval shook the circle and heads rolled on the floor and purple blood gushed out, foaming thickly.

The little girl with the shattered legs gives her long-drawn-out scream. When she dies there are plenty of children left in the camps, flocking round me with their loud anxious cries, swarming down from the roofs, slipping in through the windows and sitting on the stone benches, unwilling to believe me when I tell them that there aren't enough coloured pencils to go round at drawing time. They congregate in the Centre, pushing and shoving, and Umm Mahmoud tells them off for their unruly behaviour as they scramble over one another in their struggle to get at the pencils and the writing exercises. They draw masses of guns to defend themselves against the flash of shellfire and the heavy convulsions which they know mean that limbs will go flying through the air.

The pallor came and went, while the medical equipment performed its task unceasingly. He stirred then lapsed back into deep unconsciousness. My senses alert, I waited for him to wake up and all the possibilities to be revived. His breathing grew more regular and I felt that this was the sign I'd been waiting for, a promise exchanged that he would survive to live and breathe easily once more; that he would ponder and give his opinion and get angry, and not be choked with pain any more. His breathing grew faint and the words I was forming disappeared. Crippled, I carried the scream within me like a casualty limping on a stick into one of the field hospitals. The same sky looks down on us both through the window but he can't see it with me. Outside the cafés are bursting with customers giving their orders, and the walls are crowded with posters for new films and photographs of martyrs looking happy or sad, since they weren't able to know in advance that they should adopt poses suitable for announcing their moments of heroism.

He moved his head just a little and turned towards the corner where I was standing. It was hard to appreciate what was happening in that moment. His lower lip trembled then cleaved tightly to his upper lip. Could he really be waking up and opening his eyes? I ran to the bell and pressed it to call the nurse, as I'd been told to do, then savoured him with fearful joy and surprise because of the small movement he'd made: that he'd opened his eyes was a cause for such awe, such astonishment that it transformed the world into a little light ball flying to and fro between my fingers. With enormous weariness he looked at his dressings and tried to speak, but the nurse told him to be quiet and rest. She asked us to leave now and come back the following morning. Umm Mahmoud spread out her fingers, then curled them up and put them to her mouth. Disregarding the hospital and its trappings she let out a long trill of joy.

So he was going to live.

No, this feeling wasn't simply happiness. It was something stronger and fiercer than all the delights of life and the pleasures of victory I'd dreamt of enjoying one day. It was something different: a mixture of sun after rain, lightning flashes quivering in a black crystal sky, and particles of many scattered minutes and hours combining in a single moment. This was the moment, this was the time for life in spite of the wars, the treachery and the stabs in the back.

With the coming of night and the dark violet dusk, I felt for the first time that the city was turning towards us, flowing towards us with a sound as gentle as flocks of birds beating their wings in the air or as a headstrong arrow humming at the moment of its release. It accepted our private sorrows and joys without kicking us out of the way, and it hung photographs of its ordinary citizens and its martyrs side by side on walls which reached into the heart of the stone and the granite.

Umm Mahmoud and I looked for a car to take us back to the camp. The refreshingly cool breeze struck the sides of our faces and the closed shops and asphalted pavements raced along on either side of the street. The monotonous vibration of the car made me think of the passing of time.

'Where's it leading?' Amer says with a morose expression, his shining eyes full of dark, impenetrable sorrow: 'Arab history's a thick hair tent where repression and slow killing are perpetrated in the gloom.'

'Where's it leading?' asks Shahd, scribbling away in her exercise books. 'When will we find the joys we knew in the past again and the happiness we've sought for through the drops of sweat and the premature wrinkles on our faces? Where can I find myself if I don't stay connected with what remains of traditional femininity, when it's been reinforced in us over the past thousand years?'

'Where's it leading?' say I with a feverish shudder which sends its hot sap shooting along my veins. 'That he should live and get better is all I want now. Nothing else besides. If he's to risk death again, if I myself am, it doesn't bother me at all. All I want is to be one with the moment; it resembles all the things I own but can't see: the palm trees, the roof of Mount Qarantal casting its shadow over the Jericho sky; the blue-grey clouds; the black and white pebbles in the salty water on the Dead Sea shore; and that time which flashes and gleams between my fingers as a period of incessant waiting, or a single shot going forward to the enemy and not being returned.'

The car radio was on, and martial music fell around me like rain and slid between the seats and poured down over the windows and doors. Does music make fools of us?

'But military marches aren't music, Jinan,' Shaher says. 'They're the empty shouting of the rulers, the false claims of salesmen crying their wares in vain, a big lie that nobody but themselves believes.'

'It's the feeling of enormous heaviness as you plunge towards infinity. They're storming the aircraft. The red lights shoot around me at speed, shining on its cold metal bulk. It's this enormous heaviness weighing down my body as it begins to flow along my limbs and into my joints and my bones as they fall apart. Our bombs are exploding and taking us with them . . .'

The normal voice of a professional broadcaster announced with complete composure that the operation had ended. That's right, Salima Al-Hajja, that's how they always do it: a burning plane and a lot of dead bodies and the loud blaring of sirens. And you will surely weep with your swollen-rimmed eyes and ask, 'Did they do that to Amer as well?'

'Even to Amer.'

Amer and his degree which was hung on the prison walls and sprouted fiery, savage whips.

'And the bride I promised to him? How could he go away this time without even looking in to see me?'

They're not easy questions to answer. But Amer took his compass and his maps and a land of faded dreams and set off on board the aircraft. Everyone has his own way, Salima. He himself always said that to you.

Us and the sea.

The sea and Amer.

Amer and the aeroplanes and the long debate with history, which he would conclude only in his own way.